DEATH DEAL

JENNA KENT

Jenna is a steamy lesbian romance author of fast-paced instalove romance. Expect them to be over-the-top, absurdly ridiculous—but always with a happy ending.

1

Elena

I'm so excited for this mundane Micro Economics lecture, and I know why. Anna Stonewell will be in this class - I've heard the gossip. She has to pass this elective if she is to graduate her senior year. Most likely, this is our last chance to see her. Like all of us other love-stricken women in this classroom, I have an extra seat beside me, wishing that Anna will choose it. Could I possibly be any more desperate? I can't compete with the other wealthy classmates; but Anna's beauty leaves us all swooning as she strolls through the student recreation building. She usually wears a white t-shirt accentuating her firm breasts held up by a black bra visible through the fabric, and pairs it with black jeans hugging her curves and boots. Her thick shoulder-length dark brown hair, with streaks or auburn is often secured in a bun yet dazzling when down; she has a nose ring, piercings around her ears, and a faint coating of darker make-up. An Emo - that's what they call her - and oh my goodness do I have a major crush on Anna.

Like clockwork, she enters the room. Her expected outfit is topped with a long black cardigan, reaching her thighs. Messenger bag in hand, she beams her perfect white smile at all of us and starts up the lecture steps. We shift, throwing our bags from our chairs like desperate idiots, hoping for her to settle beside one of us - but she passes by me, and I feel stupid for feeling rejected. To my surprise, however, she sits in the row behind me, making me tuck my hair behind my ear when her sweet-smelling perfume reaches me. Her thick wavy locks flow down her shoulders today and her scent smells so divine that I can't exhale properly. Why am I so enamored by this woman? Running my hand over the back of my neck, I fluff my own long wavy dark brown hair and pull it to the side - almost as if eager to feel her warm breath brush against my neck.

I glance a couple of seats away, and I'm met with a blushing woman. Can it be? Of all people, Anna Stonewell is staring at me? She's from one of the most affluent families in this small town - billionaires who own the city. She's guarded, no doubt having many vultures attempting to take advantage of her wealth. Even the professor gives her a sultry smile when she strides in wearing her gorgeous suit. We can't help but admire Anna's beautiful features; she has a bad girl look, one that we all want a taste of. From stories at the diner, it seems like she enjoys taking beautiful women home from the local dive bar often, but there aren't any queer bars here. With her money and status, however, blind eyes are turned for her as they'd rather have her keep her wealth within this conservative area. Anna and her family is so rich, they could buy this town ten times over.

"Okay everyone, let's get started." The professor says as she hands her teaching assistant a stack of papers before passing them around the class; I know already this is the syllabus. I end up with a stack for my row, passing them around. Suddenly, I'm startled by a light tapping on my shoulder.

"Sorry, can you pass me an extra copy? Mine seems to have faded in the copy machine." Anna's lips are so close to mine, and her warm peppermint breath tickles my ear. Holy crap! I throw up my arm over my shoulder, giving her my paper as I didn't have an extra copy. Oh well, I figure I'll look it up online or ask for another copy at the end of class. Her fingers lightly brush against mine when she takes the paper from my hand; the sensation sends shivers through me.

"Thanks." She whispers into my ear, then leans back in her chair. My entire core ignites with the heat of a thousand suns and I'm sure I'm blushing like crazy. To my horror, some of the other students in my row start to quietly chuckle with laughter at me for acting silly over something as trivial as asking for an extra copy of the syllabus. But Anna isn't ordinary — her soft touch has me melting right here in my chair and daydreaming about being in bed with her all night long. With the professor dismissing us from class, I don't bother grabbing another syllabus because I'm planning never to attend this class again; instead, I plan to rush to student services tomorrow morning to switch into another lecture hall before it's too late. No way am I going back there and embarrassing myself more over Anna Stonewell — she has this inexplicable power to make me feel these sexual cravings uncontrollably!

I numb out the rest of the day, grateful that it was my only class with her. I didn't even go to the student recreation building to de-stress in between classes. I couldn't—seeing Anna there would cause me to unravel again. Why did I have such a strong reaction to this woman who doesn't even notice me? Or does she? She stared at me in class, and I felt her gaze throughout the torturous hour. No chance; I have to stay focused. Born and raised in Brookside, Michigan—a tiny, poor town—I've experienced poverty all my life. My full-ride scholarship to Northwestern University is my opportunity for escape. I'll get my Business Administration degree and get away from Brookside and Traverse City altogether; I'm thinking of relocating to Detroit and beginning anew after I graduate. Anywhere but here.

But Anna makes Traverse City worth living in. This city may be wonderful, but the cruel rich conservative snobs make this an unbearable place to exist. Thus, I'm frantically working to get out of here. As I take a break from my school activities and enjoy a small turkey sandwich at the nearby park, leisurely swinging my feet on the bench and looking around, an alarm on my phone sounds. Strangely, I feel eyes on me. I jerk and look back over my shoulder, seeing no one; feeling foolish yet, goosebumps remain on my arms and I can't shake off this eerie feeling that's lingered for the past six months. If it isn't loneliness getting the best of me, maybe I am going crazy. For years now, since I was fourteen, I've worked part-time and saved up enough money to pay for my first apartment. Subsequently, at eighteen, I quickly learnt how earning tips as a waitress can be lucrative. I'm always quick to pick up gigs at any diner I find; they're usually short-lived however given most of them are toxic work environments. Thankfully, where I currently work proves blessed reprieve from lecherous customers or worse still - co-workers or bosses – no one has tried to hit on me yet and for that I'm thankful.

Bone-tired, I stone-facedly push on. I must juggle part-time work with a demanding academic schedule—some days are a blur of lost sleep and missed meals. Yet, I soldier on; I know my hard work will pay off one day. Dutifully switching off my alarm, I quickly down my sandwich. With a lethargic sigh, I tidy up and sling my battered messenger bag over my aching shoulder. Then, I trudge off to the diner.

2

____

Anna

She senses me, my precious Elena. She knows I'm near when she turns her head while sitting peacefully on the bench, eating her turkey sandwich. Does she realize that it's me, who is always watching out for her? College has meant nothing to me until Elena Allen walked into my lecture hall last year. All my attempts to think clearly vanished and I was determined to have her. Her gorgeous olive eyes, delicate frame, and petite height of five foot five had sealed my heart to her forever. I no longer had any sense of reason. All I saw was Elena—the most exquisite thing in the world. She doesn't know how I quivered all over and my panties were dripping as class ended. I couldn't help myself today; sitting behind her gave me an opportunity to be close to her. Ordinarily, I ignore my angel purposely, not wanting any attention brought to her, but this time, I needed to feel her heat and warmth. The touch I stole when she hurriedly handed me her syllabus—which I lied about something being wrong with mine, I just needed a pretext to chat with her.

I'm stalking her from a distance, my insides writhing as she nibbles on a simple sandwich. I can't stand that she's not eating enough, but I have to keep my distance until the time is right. Elena is everything to me - my entire universe. She doesn't understand the adoration I bear for her and frankly, I've abandoned attempts at understanding this fixation I have with her. I need her like air to breathe, plain and simple. Elena stands, pushing back her delectable locks which I crave to bury my face in behind her shoulders and snatches her messenger bag, glancing around for the stalker which has raised the hair on her arms, warning her someone is watching. That creepy stalker is me; it's been me for the past six months when I purchased her apartment complex so I can enter secretly and without causing a stir, usually in the middle of the night to watch her sleep for a few hours and explore her living space. Other evenings while she's working at the diner, I'll slip into her bed and savor her sweet aroma or can be found rummaging through her underwear drawer.

Elena Allen belongs to me—she just doesn't know it yet. I've made sure that everyone else, especially her sleazeball boss, Jordan, knows better. As I follow her, I'm trying to figure out who the real monster is—me or him? When I discovered he'd been watching her change through a peephole in the diner's public restroom, I nearly ripped his head off. And when he started trailing her home after her shift, I cornered him for a little chat. The minute she quits that job, he's a dead man; until then, threatening and warning him has been enough to terrify him. He pissed himself when I walked him to the lake's lighthouse and threatened to blow his brains out. But he still doesn't have the balls to challenge me—a Stonewell whose family has been in the crime business since we migrated from Italy in the early twentieth century.

I'm a monster, but the darkness that Elena Allen evokes in me far exceeds my expectations. I love her with all of my heart, mind, body, and soul. As she strides across the street into town, entering the diner opposite from the Great Wolf Lodge Hotel, which is usually packed with tourists around this time of year—and tonight is no exception. She'll probably be exhausted by the end of the night; I should think of a way to cut the power in the area so that she can go straight home and rest. Just as I plan out a way to do this with my wealth and power, my phone starts to ring; it's my brother Angelo, always calling at an inconvenient time. Frustrated, I answer gruffly: "What?"

"Stop harassing that innocent girl and return to your usual conquests. They've even dropped by the mansion, confused as to why you're avoiding them." I groan into the phone. I've firmly announced that all our arrangements have been terminated. No public shows of begging and groveling are allowed; my female companions know better than to provoke my rage. But showing up at my door without permission...I can feel the flames licking within me, but I must stay in control. There's too much left behind for me to risk a jail sentence—especially without Elena's presence.

"Inform them to scram and I'll handle them later," I snarl into the phone, ready to hang up, when Angelo interjects:

"Your father requires you at the estate for a family meeting. It's mandatory."

"Shit." I snarl, "I'm on my way." I hang up the call and take one last look at my sweetheart fading away into the diner. Desperate for her to be happy, wishing I could comfort her from her suffering, but all I can do is wait—wait until it's the correct time. Elena loves school and her education more than her mental health, which has grown weaker over time. She doesn't participate in any fun activities or make friends; she just works, sleeps, cleans and takes a day of rest each Sunday dedicated to cooking a large crock pot meal that will feed her through the week. I've tried slipping cash under her door to help ease her burden, but she only gives it away to an elderly woman in her building who should be in a senior facility. My sweetheart always puts others before herself, but what she doesn't know is that I plan on putting myself ahead of her. Elena will be adored and have every desire fulfilled. All I want is for her to love me; I need her to love me.

And so far, I think she does. As Elena slips out of view behind the diner counter, I walk away from the street corner back to the park's parking lot to my car.

3

Anna

Driving home to the family mansion has me in a sour mood. There must be a meaningful purpose for this mandatory family meeting. I had just left my sweetheart alone, unwatched, to attend this meeting that I'm usually not called for. I am not pleased with it in the slightest. Driving into Bayshore, the subdivision where my family mansion resides, I quickly roll down my driver's window so security can view me and let me pass. My father is the founder of this guarded community and he keeps it heavily fortified. We have surveillance everywhere. I'm thinking about asking my father for two individual guards to watch over Elena whenever I'm not close to her, but I don't want to intimidate her. Yet she needs my protection. If Angelo knows that I'm tracking Elena, then that means my father knows as well. Is that why he's summoned me?

Pulling into the extended driveway, I groan when Arnold, the butler of my father's estate stands outside waiting for me. Damn, this must be significant. As soon as I stop, Arnold strides around to the driver's side door and opens it for me, proffering his hand for me to exit. I've known Arnold since infancy; he's been a steadfast member of our family.

"How serious is the situation?" I enquire. He smirks back at me with an air of superiority.

"It's a family emergency, madam. You'll find everyone in your father's study." I furrow my brows in annoyance. Arnold knows how much I dislike it when he calls me that pretentious title, yet he continues to do it anyway - just one of his many quirks. He's been offered promotions every year and turns them down without hesitation; being a butler and ruling over the help here at the mansion gives him too much pleasure. Despite not being related by blood, I consider Arnold part of my family and cannot imagine living another day without him.

While Arnold climbs into my car, I head up the stairs to the double front doors while he parks it in the garage. Pulling out my phone, I keep a close eye on the time to ensure that my sweetheart returns home safely. Thoughts of her consume me and render me incapable of functioning until she is safe.

Surprise hits me as soon as I enter the study; not only did I find my father, but his two sons Angelo and Aberto. Aberto's presence takes me aback: why would he be here? He detests our family's heritage since his departure ten years ago to pursue his doctorate studies. His aspiration had sparked mine to break away from the clutches of our Stonewell family. I am the only daughter, and my mother died of cancer when I was four. My father refuses to accept my lesbianism, making it challenging for him to use marriage as an act of diplomacy with his adversaries.

Aberto cheerfully greets me upon seeing me. Our

communication has been limited to video chats over the years. His attendance here implies a serious matter. With my hands behind my back, I step in, putting on an evil smile. Something is amiss, but I do not want to waste any time playing games; rather, I would like to move onto more important issues such as stalking Elena.

"Anna, take a seat." My father directs, motioning to the empty spot on the couch, beside my brothers. I roll my eyes in response and oblige because the sooner it's over, the better.

"Why did you summon me?" I probe. As I'm never invited to family meetings. My father takes a patriarchal stance that women are homemakers and I blatantly disregard his standards, which infuriates him; so, he was quick to buy a house closer to the university and evict me due to my sexuality. Our relationship is strained, to say the least, as we can't bear being around each other for more than a few minutes without bickering. He relaxes into his chair once I sit next to Aberto without confronting him. Just like my father, I'm always ready for a fight and never bow out of any confrontations.

"Father, why did you summon us?" Aberto enquires, still wearing his lab coat. He must have hurriedly driven up here after work. My father clears his throat and Arnold walks in shortly afterwards, to which my father gestures for him to bring him a drink; Arnold nods in understanding, as he already knows what my father likes to indulge in. Arnold is also aware of everyone's preferences, even Aberto's, despite the fact that it has been more than ten years since he left the family.

"It's time for me to retire. I'm leaving the business," my father announces gravely. Gasps of shock fill the room and I am just as taken aback as everyone else - we all know what this means. If my father is to leave his professional life of crime behind then it could only mean that he is planning on going off the grid. His line of business is far too deep in criminality for this not to be true, and I'm certain those powerful mafia criminals he made death deals with are far from pleased with his decision.

Aberto sighs heavily and places his hands on his lap; his face contorted with anger at the realization that today had finally come. Just like me, he never thought this day would actually arrive so he had resigned himself to the fate of being a Stonewell forever.

"I have invested the last decade of my life into my career, Father. You now decide it is time for us to go off the grid? What about my accomplishments and potential family I have built?" My father accepts a drink from Arnold, and motions for him to serve the rest of us. Angelo looks content with this decision. As for me, I am unsure what to make of this revelation. I understand that if I remain here, bounties will be placed on our heads - including mine - and we must hide not only from the authorities but from vicious assassins seeking to take our lives. A death warrant will be issued against my father, from the mafia criminals who wish to eliminate his bloodline: my brother's wives and their children, as well as me. I cannot stay once my father vanishes; I must leave with him. But can I depart without Elena? The thought causes an agonizing ache in my heart. No; I must find a way to bring her with me. Without Elena, there's no life for me.

"Then you must find a way to bring your family with you. On the provision that I leave for the island by the end of this week, you have four days to make arrangements. The private jet departs Friday at midnight and will not return until Sunday evening. You'll join me, or you'll stay, but I won't take on the burden of your decision. Because we all know if you choose to stay, you'll die. And I won't weep for any of you if you choose to stay."

My father takes a sip of his dark beverage before looking me in the eyes, wearing an eerie smile.

"Are you concerned for the Allen girl, Anna? I know how much she means to you." Bile rises in my throat as I glare daggers at him, realizing he has been observing me watching her all this time.

"I have a dossier on the Allen girl too; since you bought her apartment building of course! Why don't you just ask her out? She is very beautiful and seemingly naïve. Too naive for a Stonewell if I should be honest."

"Your opinion matters little to me!" I spit back and hear him chuckle.

"You remind me so much of myself, Anna. I watched your mother for a year before she was finally worn down; yielding to my desires. It seems like you are doing exactly the same now." Angelo's snickering only infuriates me further, but Aberto soothes me with a gentle touch on my shoulder. He's the only one who seems to understand me.

"If you wish to bring her, then do so. But bear in mind the trials that await her. And understand how you will spend the rest of your life trying to keep her alive. Is it self-interest Anna, like your father? Will you force this woman with her entire life ahead of her into your world simply because you can't go without?" I want to hurl something at him, yet Aberto's iron grip on my shoulder stops me. There it is: the harsh truth – the reality I have no choice but to confront. Can I do it? Can I be unselfish and leave without Elena?

No. I cannot. And I won't.

4

——————

Elena

Two Days Later

Anna hadn't shown up to our economics lecture, and I was quite bothered by it. I hadn't seen her on campus since Monday, and I couldn't help but worry if something was wrong. Why did I have to be such a crazy girl-fan over this woman who was clearly out of my league? I can't understand the strong desires I have for this woman, yet I still miss her; she brightens even my darkest days with a simple glimpse at her beautiful face. Now it's just me, work, and the pressure of my studies plus meeting deadlines. I'm working at the diner, feeling melancholic as I wipe off tables in this abandoned place. It's Wednesday night, always dead here on Wednesdays; I'm barely getting paid for it and tips give almost nothing. Jordan's been acting weird with me lately, saying only a few words and asking others to tell me what to do instead of directing me himself. Is he about to fire me? Oh no, another job search is something that can wait until the end of the semester. My budget is already so tight; losing this job now would really hurt me. I put my hand over my chest, wondering if I can handle any more stress. All I want is a day off, not my typical Sundays where I'm merely prepping for the next week. Even then, I still feel drained, doing chores, cooking meals and running errands.

Startled, I hear the bell from the diner door jingle. Quickly, I finish wiping the table and grab some menus and silverware sets. When I turn around, my heart stops for a second. Anna stands before me looking more stunning than ever, her wavy hair cascading over her shoulders as her long black cardigan is paired with fitted jeans and a T-shirt. She slides into the booth, fiddling with the rings on her fingers while averting her gaze from me. It's Wednesday so I'm the only waitress on rotation. Taking a deep breath, I move towards Anna and place a menu in front of her with the silverware settings. Self-consciously I pull out my notepad to take her order but pause when she looks up at me with a soft smile.

"Elena, how are you?" I almost can't believe it when she says my name; the sound of her soft voice loops in my ears. She knows my name. My lips part but no words come out. She giggles lightly and opens the menu.

"Good, I guess?" She answers for me and I have to clear my throat. My eyes catches sight of her beautifully painted navy-blue nails - not the usual black coating. I probably have been staring too hard as she pulls one of her hands from the menu to examine her nails.

"The nail technician suggested a different color this

time, not always black. Maybe that will capture my love interests attention this time." I blink a few times then stare into her eyes - my heart falling at that piece of information. A love interest... wow. My jealousy becomes difficult to contain.

"She's a lucky woman." I breathe out, regret panging in my chest. How foolish I am to believe there was a chance with this woman; Anna's more than likely interested in someone she has known for some time and must have a history with.

"Don't look so glum, Elena." Anna speaks, further fueling the fire in me - anger and jealousy tangling together like a tornado inside me. I let out a huff, fighting against tears as reality set in: I am an idiot for thinking Anna has any interest in me.

"Can I take your order? How about something to drink to start?" My voice sounds shaky even to me.

"Oh, Elena," she breathes, setting the menu down. Then she surprises me by grabbing my wrist and scooting over, pulling me close beside her into the booth. A tear escapes my eye, rolling down my face. She catches it and tenderly strokes her finger across my cheek.

"You're so strange, Elena. Why are you crying?" I shake my head, avoiding her gaze.

"I think I'm overwhelmed with school and work." It's a partial truth; the only way I can explain my reaction. I close my eyes, inhaling the sweet scent of her perfume—a tropical aroma that draws me in. What is it? I swear I dream about it and sometimes I can smell it on my pillow when I'm sleeping. She continues to gently rub my shoulders and the soft touch of her makes me dizzy almost. Trying to compose myself, I shake my head.

"I'm sorry to be this waitress who can't seem to hold it together." Even though I joke, she doesn't laugh; instead, she keeps rubbing my arms, gazing at me with concern.

"What's really bothering you, Elena?" she asks but I can't answer because all that'll do is make me look foolish. No way! My crush on her will stay buried deep inside me forever. Anna is so beautiful and everything I ever dreamed of in a woman; she's everything I want...but it's impossible for someone like me. Maybe once college ends and I move away to Detroit there might be someone out there who could fill these big shoes...but until then Anna will remain in a special place in my heart.

"Would it make you feel better if I ordered a drink?" she asks, her beautiful light brown eyes locking with mine. Her luscious pink lips, coated with lip gloss, curves into a smile, and I almost lose control - leaning in to kiss her.

"Alright," she chuckles lightly, "I'll have an ice-tea, unsweetened." Gently pulling away from her gaze, I slide out of the booth and dash off to fetch the drink. A quick splash of cold water over my face and a few slaps later, I make my way back towards her. She beams warmly at me and pats the empty space next to her for me to sit down again.

"Why don't you join me for a sec?" I shake my head nervously, knowing that another second in this close proximity to the woman of my dreams will send me overboard.

"I can't. I'm on the clock. I don't want to piss my boss off." Hardly spoken words come from Jordan behind me; he has barely uttered anything to me before now.

"Hey Elena, it's pretty dead today so you can finish up that customer you have then clock out." I groan inwardly as Anna's smile widens even further; but when I glance at Jordan, his eyes are on Anna - uneasy and unsure.

"I'll just have this drink. Let me pay for it, so you can finish your shift and join me." She fishes out a twenty from her pocket and hands it to me with an eager expression. I swallow hard, take the money, then walk over to the register to ring up her order. After setting her change down on the counter, I clock out in the back and quickly change into my own clothes - a tank-top, light sweater, and sweatpants - in the women's restroom.

"Keep that as a tip." She says when I return to the table, sliding the coins towards me.

"No way," I shake my head, that beverage only cost two dollars – I hardly earned a tip that size!

"Shall I put it in your pocket myself?" Anna smirks suggestively at me. "Or do you prefer to keep your money in your bra?"

Oh crap! Is she flirting with me? My cheeks burn as I accept the change and stuff it into my pocket. It doesn't help that I smell like beef and cheese sliders - surely not appealing! Anna finishes her tea before speaking again.

"I don't think it was the drink that brought me here." Her eyes move slowly over my body before settling on my lips; I lick them unconsciously as realization set in: she's come here for me.

"Me?" I point at myself in disbelief. Is she asking for help with her homework or something? She had missed a day of classes after all.

"Yes, Elena. I want to do something special for a woman like you—to show you the respect and kindness you deserve."

Wait, what? I gulp and stare at her inquisitively, waiting for clarification.

"I'd like to take you out on a date. Will you go out with me?" My jaw drops in shock; Anna Stonewell wants to take me on a date? I'm dumbfounded, unable to contain my enthusiastic response.

"YES!" I exclaim loudly, reverberating across the now-empty diner. Anna laughs and takes my hand, bringing it up to her lips for a gentle kiss.

"Good, that makes me very happy," she says warmly.

"I've been wanting to ask you out for a while now, but I get nervous around you." I shake my head in disbelief, blushing deeply.

"No way," I respond shyly. "A plain girl like me?" She laughs in response.

"Yes, Elena," she insists confidently. "You're more stunning than any other woman I've ever met." I gasp at these words, feeling my heart rate quicken with every passing moment.

"When would you like to go out? We can meet somewhere if that works better for you."

"How about right now?" Suddenly, my smile fades into confusion as reality sets in.

"But it's already evening of a rather dull Wednesday night—what could we possibly do?" She gives me a sultry look and raises an eyebrow in question. Damn, she sure knows how to get what she wants....

"Are you saying no, Elena?" I rapidly shake my head, still taken aback by her suggestion. She chuckles in response.

"Good. Let's take you home. Change into something nice. I'll take you out for dinner, then I'd like to take you dancing."

"But we have school tomorrow." I remind her. Anna shrugs.

"You look like you could use a day off from the world. There's nothing wrong with self-care, Elena." Her words hit me like a ton of bricks. How long have I waited for a moment like this? Just time for myself, to relax and rest? I nod then slide out of the booth, Anna doesn't let go of my hand as she slides out, then takes my messenger bag from me and walks me out of the diner, taking me to her car.

$$5$$

Anna

Elena opens the door to her tiny apartment, and I follow in close behind as she rushes around attempting to tidy. With all the basic amenities, the apartment is overly priced, but I haven't lowered the rent when I bought the building- all so she wouldn't get suspicious and investigate the new owner. She pulls a chair from the small table and offers me a seat. Her studio apartment is small; containing only a full-sized bed, television, and dressers. Plus, two book shelves and a tiny table for two. Though no sofa is present; where would she fit one? In the kitchen sits a stove, fridge, microwave with her favorite crock pot on the countertop. I've been in her apartment many times before, though she doesn't know that or of the monitoring system I had installed while she was away in classes. Placing myself in the chair, my eyes observe her kick off her shoes and rush to her closet; searching for that beautiful blue dress I want to marry her in. Impatiently licking my lips, I watch as she retrieves it and holds it up to herself -

wondering if it still fits. Lowering my gaze to my nails which are also painted blue, I wonder why she's so fond of this color above all others. She looks back at me holding the dress before smiling.

"That's perfect. I intend on taking you somewhere that oozes class tonight, and your dress will be the cherry on top." Her cheeks blush as she glances down at the dress.

"I love the color blue, just like your beautiful painted nails," I beam with delight, knowing this fact about her. It's why I painted my own nails in matching shades of blue – I enjoy black over any other color, but for Elena, I love what she loves.

"Get dressed, I'll wait." I command. She blushes and grabs some fresh underwear before scurrying off to the bathroom and shutting the door. The sound of water cascading down followed by a clatter of objects echoes in my ears. With resolve, I nestle into the chair across from her full-sized bed. Soon enough, I'll be telling her that accepting to date me means giving up her freedom forever. This will be the last night she'll ever be alone. Elena has no idea what awaits her and I must cement my hold on her before we leave this place for good. But something about Traverse City doesn't quite sit well with her. Her fascination with my father's area is evident from her search history. It appears that she too has done her research and is just as obsessed with me as I am with her. What dark thoughts does she harbor for me? What twisted fantasies has she conjured up while pleasuring herself? My mind races at the possibilities as I recall the scent of her arousal and how it intoxicated me every time I buried my face in her sheets. I know who I am - a sick asshole with no qualms about getting what I want - but somehow that realization doesn't matter anymore because all that matters now is Elena and making sure she's mine forever.

My passionate craving for her can only be sated by her presence. Yet she's still inside the bathroom, trying desperately to look perfect for me. What she did not understand was that she's already immaculate in my eyes. I'd prefer to relish in her nudity rather than seeing her stressing out over getting ready.

Nonetheless, my current priority is getting her out as soon as possible. This will be the last time she sets foot into this apartment; and I know she may despise me for making these decisions, but I will attempt to win back her heart in due course.

After about twenty minutes, she emerges from the bathroom, her hair tousled and her beautiful blue dress tugged over her hips. Damn, she looks stunningly gorgeous! My gaze follows her as she glides to the dresser and opens it to take out a pair of earrings and jewelry. I've never seen Elena so dressed up for anyone - not even during holidays when she'd have to travel to Brookside to visit her mother. Sadly, her mother has always shown strong disapproval of Elena's sexuality and had sent men over in an effort to change her mind - something that ceased when I came into the picture. I've threatened to kill the last two men her mother had sent. As Elena finishes getting ready, my mouth waters with anticipation; I am eager to explore every inch of her body. Finally, she turns around and I am awestruck by her beauty - my expectations completely exceeded! My jaw drops open as she timidly walks up to me, hands anxiously gripping her belly. Jesus, she is breathtaking.

The dress clings to her curves, her breasts practically spilling out. I can tell she's gained weight since the last time she wore it, and it looks good on her— too good. How old is this thing? She must have been malnourished when she bought it; not eating enough for my taste.

"Is this okay?" she asks me and I gulp. It's enough to make me forget about dinner and take her straight to bed, but I have a plan. The moment we leave this apartment, my plan will come to motion and she'll be mine forever—a fate I'm looking forward to.

"Elena, perfection isn't the word I'd use," I murmur, my hand finding its way to her bare thigh, her skin warm beneath me. I ache to have my head between her legs, feeling her warmth encasing me. She gasps but doesn't move away from me; so fucking beautiful.

Surprisingly, she leans in, seemingly enjoying the caress of my fingers as I admire her flesh. My mouth is watering, my heart is pounding, my entire body is on fire.

"I think we should get out of here." I tell her and she smiles, taking a step back. My fingers ache from the loss of contact with her thigh. My eyes follow her like a hawk as she strides to the closet to grab a long sweater and slip on some small flats before coming back to me. She grabs a small purse and her keys, throwing them over her shoulder.

"Alright, I'm ready." She says, waiting for me. I rise from the chair and follow her out the door; patiently awaiting as she locks it securely before leaving. I take her hand and she blushes, strolling down the stairs of her apartment, out of the building and back to my car. I open the passenger door for her and once inside, I take one final look at the apartment building knowing it's going back up for sale tomorrow after I call the moving service I have contracted to pack up Elena's belongings. Her place is with me - until our days come to an end.

6

____

Elena

I groan when Anna pulls us in front of Pedro's, one of the top fine dining restaurants in Traverse City. I couldn't even get a job here as a waitress because even their waitstaff are high end and middle class. I was told I didn't have "the look" for the position which meant I looked too poor. Too poor to wear the staff uniform? I let out a loud huff once she pulls in front of the valet, folding my arms over my chest, scowling at the building.

"Is there a problem, Elena? Are you not a fan of this restaurant? It's the best in town, but if you'd prefer someplace else, I'll gladly oblige." Anna says, staring at me with concern. I look to her nervously, not realizing I am pouting and sulking over the memory of my humiliating interview here. The hiring manager made me feel so low that day. I let out a breath and shake my head.

"No, it's sweet that you brought me here. Sorry, just had a bad memory is all." Anna smirks and opens her door before quickly coming around to help me out of the passenger side.

"Elena, please don't take this the wrong way, but let me cater to you tonight, okay?" I awkwardly stare at her, understanding what she means. Anna wants to open my doors, help me to my chairs, and possibly cut my meat and feed it to me. She wants to pamper me; it's something higher class women demand, but I'm used to taking care of myself. I nod and smile because I'm so happy to be in her company. Nothing is stopping me from being here on this date instead of at home prepping for school. Even if I miss the first half of my day due to exhaustion—I can't pass up this opportunity that I've been begging for over a year.

"Anna," a beautiful hostess speaks, eying her seductively. I gulp, looking away and examining my dress—wondering if I look ridiculous in this high-end restaurant. With Anna's wealth and affluence, there will be no issue with any dress code; they would never deny her entry anywhere. But as casually as the hostess treats Anna, I can't help but feel jealous. Do they have a past? Maybe lovers? My curiosity overwhelms me.

"Alexa, good to see you." I take a step back and snatch my hand away from Anna when Alexa comes from behind the podium to greet her. She pulls her into a hug and plants a kiss on both sides of her cheeks. Anna welcomes her quickly, but pulls back, scowling at me as I look away nervously. She grabs my hand, pulling me back to her side. Alexa's attention is caught; she eyes me suspiciously.

"Got a date, I see." she says, eying me up and down. It makes me feel uncomfortable.

"Nice dress," she murmurs, but it's not a compliment. It's more like a dig on my appearance. I try to tug my hand away so I can close my cardigan, but Anna won't release me. Instead, she pulls my hand to her lips right in front of Alexa, kissing the back of it.

"Yes, for now she's, my date. But I'm hoping it becomes more than that. This is Elena." Without a reservation, Anna continues proudly. "It's a slow night; could you squeeze us into a booth?" Alexa glares at me as if she wants to deny Anna – but she doesn't. She lets out a sigh and turns back towards the podium, grabbing two menus.

"Of course, Anna – no way am I gonna deny a Stonewell; I'll get fired on the spot." She winks, leading the way through the restaurant. Anna holds my hand tightly as we walk with pride until Alexa stops at a booth and places the menus down. Anna makes sure I'm seated first before she slides into the booth across from me.

"Order anything you like. The seafood is delicious – I highly recommend it." She tells me. I scan the menu, unsure of what I want. Never have I been to such a high-class restaurant; working at the diner grants me only the occasional crockpot meal or turkey sandwich if I manage to save enough tips from working. This menu is nothing like the diner's. Maybe just a soup?

"When was the last time you had a decent steak? The grade of their meat is pretty good, not perfect though." I shrug, not meeting her gaze. Prices are nowhere to be seen here - this place is insanely expensive. It seems that Anna notices my apprehension as she takes the menu away and says, "It's okay, Elena. You can order whatever you want. Don't be shy around me."

"I'm poor..." I blurt out nervously as other diners start to stare at me. Lowering my voice, I apologize for being ill-mannered in such a nice establishment, "I'm sorry; I don't know how to act in a place like this. Jesus, even the fish tank that's holding the lobsters for cooking looks fancy." Anna smiles at me.

"Elena, do you think I give a damn about that? I asked you out because I think you're gorgeous and charming. I want to get to know you better. Do you care about my wealth?" I swiftly shake my head. It's accurate; I don't care how much money she has, but it would be a lie if I said it wasn't a reflection. Her money only bothers me since I recognize that I'll never fit in with her. Anna reclines in her seat, never losing eye contact with me when the waitress shows up to take our order. And of course, she has her eyes on Anna as well.

"Samantha, good seeing you." Anna states, but she doesn't make eye contact with the server. Damn, she's been intimate with her too?

"What are you having?" She asks, clutching her notepad.

"We'll have your most expensive bottle of wine and two surf and turf dinners, medium well done." Anna places the orders for me and I'm thankful that she does. I'm too flustered and a bit anxious for the wine because I could really use a swig of something. They didn't card me and Anna is over twenty-one so it's okay for her to order the bottle.

"Why did you ask me out?" I can't help it; I'm dying to know. The waitress brings the bottle of wine and two glasses. Anna pours them for me and I hastily take a sip, anxious that they'll card me and find out that I'm only twenty.

"Take it easy on that, Elena. This is a really strong brand. I don't want you inebriated before your meal arrives." I nervously place my glass down on the table and she smiles.

"Why not, Elena? I thought to myself it was now or never — it was time for me to stop watching you from afar, wishing I could have a moment alone with you and just take a chance." I gulp, my heart racing. She's been watching me?

"How long have you been wanting to ask me out?"

"A while, sweetheart."

"But whenever I saw you on campus, you'd always look right past me." Her light eyes sparkle as she smiles at me. "I was trying to spare you, sweetheart." I narrow my eyes at her, but before I can ask anything else the waitress returns with some bread, making small talk with Anna.

"I tried calling you a few times, but you never picked up." She shrugs, not taking her eyes off of me. Feeling nervous, I grab some of the bread and stuff it into my mouth. Quite unexpectedly, the woman in front of me is beautiful — even in her upscale waitress uniform; her long straight blonde hair frames her curvy waistline and delicate face features topped off by an enchanting smile that refuses to look at me. It's as if I don't exist here in this moment. She only has eyes for Anna.

"I made it clear to you last time we spoke that I was done with the bachelorette lifestyle — I'm looking to settle down." As she says this, Anna's eyes pierce mine, as if searching for an answer hidden deep within my soul. Settle down? Does she want to settle down with me?

"But really," Samantha pleads softly with Anna. "I just want to talk; have a chat about some things."

"Now's not the time," she quickly declines. "I'm on a very special date right now."

"Would you please answer the phone when I call you later?" Samantha's heartache for Anna is obvious, and it seems Anna has just tossed her aside. Will I feel this broken-hearted for Anna once she's finished with me? So many questions running through my mind. What does she mean by "settle down"?

"Certainly, Samantha. I'll answer your call and give you a minute of my time. Later." Samantha breathes out a deep breath of relief then vanishes from our table. Anna's gaze never leaves mine.

"I apologize for that disturbance. I told her six months ago that I wanted to move on from the single life." I glare at her with suspicion. Six months ago? What had she been doing between then and now, before she asked me out?

7

———

Anna

Our little date just keeps getting more captivating. Elena stares at me, her expression one of befuddlement. Would she like to know the truth? I ache to tell her. Six months ago, I was feverishly buying her apartment building in hopes of being near her. Six months ago, I started entering her home when she was in a deep slumber, standing over her, softly stroking her face, inhaling her hair, fixating over her, longing that I could join her in bed and lay my head on her succulent breasts that practically have me drooling as they look as if they are going to burst through that exquisite blue dress. I lick my lips, gazing at her salaciously. Despite being hungry, I don't want any of this food. I'd rather devour her instead - something I plan on doing later tonight.

"Settling down? Did you say that just so she'd go away?" I shake my head. I'd prefer to dodge answering the question presently since the last thing I want is for her to be suspicious of me. Elena is mine, whether she desires it or not, but thankfully fortune might be on my side now, because she appears interested in me, even jealous. First with Alexa, now with Samantha. My darling is possessive. Perfection! I grin, watching her as she shifts in her seat, gnawing angrily on the bread, attempting not to glance into my eyes.

"No, darling." She reddens at my intimate term for her, "I meant what I said to her. I'm looking to settle down."

"But you broke up with her six months ago? Were you seeing someone else then?" I smirk at the jealousy oozing out from her tone. She's got nothing to be jealous of. Elena had me captured from the moment I laid eyes on her. She stole my heart, body and soul, alluring me with a captivating smile.

"No, Elena. No one but you." I reassure her. Samantha arrives with our meals and I could take a few bites as I am hungry, though the way she forcefully shoves my plate toward me deters me from eating it. Could she have poisoned Elena's food due to envy? Elena notices my hesitation and I take her plate, swapping it with my own.

"I didn't lace anything in the food or whatever if that's what you were thinking." Samantha retorts, folding her arms.

"Glad to hear it, Samantha. Because messing with me isn't something you want to do right now." I wink at Elena and Samantha stalks off. She really begins to grate on my nerves, hindering my date, thwarting my plan. One more stop for a dance, then I'm taking Elena home with me to seduce her just enough so she submits to me.

My father is right about me; I'm no different from him when it comes to craving Elena; criminally obsessed for this woman over the past year, shielding her from danger while searching for ways to get closer to her, yet I never advanced things between us.

"If you liked me all this time, Anna," Liked? Hell no! I don't just like Elena; I love her madly and desperately.

"Why didn't you ask me out? You've acted as if I'm irrelevant, barely even noticing me."

"I was trying to protect you, Elena. I adore you in a way that even I fear." I'm honest with her this time, as I need her to end this suspiciousness. It's ridiculous and could make me expose my plan and tell her everything. The way I am entranced by her, the smell of her scent, lusting for the taste of her pussy on my lips. Does she want to be aware of the full degree of my mania? Can she manage it? I'd rather keep that part for when I take her to my father's plane Friday night.

"Protect me from what? Is it because I'm poor?" I glare at her.

"That's enough, Elena. Eat your food." Her answer startles me. She sighs heavily, still glaring at me, and takes hold of her knife and fork, cutting into her steak. She complies. Interesting, it was not something that I had anticipated. That only increases my cravings for her. What do I need to do to have her compliance? Anything she needs is hers if she gives herself completely to me, trusts me with all her wants and needs fully met. Does she not realize how much temptation she is giving me right now? How much I want her right now? She looks at me between bites, and it is quite possibly the cutest thing I've ever seen.

"You said you want to get to know me better? What do you want to know?" she asks, her voice quavering. I already know this woman better than she knows herself. For the past six months I have heavily monitored her desires and passions including tracking her periods; they are always on the fifteenth of the month, and she's always grouchy and fatigued a week before it starts. She loves chocolate, blue is her favorite color, and she hates wearing heels. Plus, she developed an infatuation for me though I am not her initial crush—before me there had been another woman in high school, but sadly Elena's heart was shattered after finding out that the woman wasn't gay. Nevertheless, there was something I ache to ask. I want to understand just how deep are her feelings for me.

"How do you feel about me, Elena?" I query, watching as she stiffens while holding her fork to her mouth. Smiling so softly, I notice that my question isn't one she anticipated.

"Uh—um," she mutters nervously, rapidly shoving the utensil into her mouth to dodge speaking. As I smile at her foolishness, she nervously gulps down some wine then exhales heavily while gazing unwaveringly into my eyes.

"Is it that bad, Elena?" Her uneasiness grows as I question her further; taking another sip of wine before continuing.

"I've wanted you for a long time, Anna—longer than six months." Aching to communicate to her how those words accelerated my heartbeat, suppressing the urge to rush over to her side of the booth and snatch her close to me with a passionate embrace; instead, my hands curl under the table digging my nails deep into my thigh through the thick fabric of my jeans until it almost hurt too much to bear any longer.

"Why didn't you say anything, Elena?" I would have jumped at the chance if she had made a move on me. I've wanted her for as long and I've been tracking her closely for the last six months - my obsession with her only growing stronger by the day. But am I like my father? I'm determined to have this woman, plotting to steal her away from her world, her hard work and dedication to school, so that I can keep her all to myself.

Shaking those thoughts out of my head, my objectives are clear: take Elena with me when I leave.

"I was afraid you'd turn me down. I'm from Brookside, Anna. I'm practically poor. I'm surprised you even asked me out on a date. It's not as if I could measure up to the other women you usually spend time with." Her beautiful olive eyes scan over to Samantha who is wiping a table nearby and clearly listening in on our conversation. I made a mistake bringing her here; it's distracting me from spending quality time with Elena.

"You were wrong, Elena. I would never have turned you down." My gaze lingers on Samantha before finally returning back to Elena's face. It wasn't until she came into my life that I realized what real love was - that genuine yearning for companionship. And now, more than ever, I want it all from her.

"If I had, would someone else be in this booth? Would I end up like her?" Elena murmurs, glancing at Samantha. I suppress a chuckle; it's a ridiculous notion. Elena is no play-thing to me--she'll be my future wife. With that thought, I hold my hand out for the check, eager to get us out of here.

"But you haven't touched your food. And I know this stuff is expensive." Her eyes narrow. I shrug nonchalantly, not caring one bit about the cost or wastefulness. "I'll take it home with me if it pleases you, Elena. But now, let's move on to the next step of our date if you don't mind."

"What's that?" She queries me, and I beam at her.

"I'd love to take you dancing." Step two of my plan: dinner, dancing, fucking, then marriage. No questions asked--Elena was mine the moment she stepped outside her apartment with me.

8

____

Elena

Samantha passes Anna the check, along with a take-out box. Anna begins packing up her food while I stare straight at her. Dancing? What exactly is so important about going out to dance? Honestly, I'm exhausted and not in the mood to visit another venue where I would have to deal with another one of Anna's exes. Besides, it's been a long day of school and work. Finishing this delicious meal made me want nothing more than to climb into bed and cuddle with Anna.

"Anna, I think it's sweet that you want to take me dancing and everything, but do you think we could rain-check on that?" I say remorsefully. She narrows her eyes at me as she pulls her card out of her wallet to pay the bill. Samantha quickly takes the bill and card and walks off to settle the balance.

Do you really want to know how much all this cost? I think to myself as a bead of sweat trickles down my forehead.

"Why? This date is special to me. I want us both to have a good time," Anna explains in a serious tone.

Feeling a bit guilty for ruining her plans, I reach over the table and grab her hand tightly. Her touch sends shivers down my spine.

I can see how much this date means to her reflected in her eyes as she brushes our intertwined fingers together softly. It makes me realize how easy it was for her to get me wrapped around her finger. It also reminds me of how much I love her.

She gives me a small smile despite the disappointment lurking behind those beautiful light brown eyes that I often find myself getting lost in.

No, I can't let her be disappointed in me. Not when I love her this much.

"Alright, Elena, but I'm not taking you home—I'm keeping you." She winks and my mouth drops open. Holy hell, this is becoming harder to deal with; I can't say no to her. I nod instead, and she doesn't let go of my hand as we make our way to Samantha. I can't bear to look at the beautiful, forlorn woman as she returns Anna's card to her.

"I'll call you," Samantha says pleadingly. But Anna clasps my hand tighter, almost as if wanting me to know she chooses me. It's a choice I want her to make: I want her to choose me. Yet I wonder if someday I'll be in Samantha's position, begging her to take my calls.

"I'll answer," Anna reassures Samantha as she steps around her, tugging me after her. We walk through the restaurant towards the exit and find Anna's car already waiting for us outside. Wow...this place really knows how to treat her well. She helps me into the car before tipping the valet then gets in the driver's side and drives off. I watch nervously, quietly as she takes me through town.

"If you aren't taking me home...where are we going?" I ask her. A proud smile forms on her face when we stop at a light.

"Let's go somewhere quiet where we can talk and I can get that dance from you." She answers, and my jaw drops. She drives me to the university park, which is deserted at this hour, parking in the lot without turning off the engine. Soft music tumbles from the radio as she rolls down the windows. When she steps out of the car, I wait for her to walk around and open my door, then she tugs me towards the front of the car where her headlights illuminated us, drawing me into her embrace.

"I'd love to dance with you, Elena." She pulls me close, swaying us slowly from side to side; our lips just inches away from each other. Anna is a woman that gets what she wants and tonight I'm giving her the dance she asked for. The cool autumn air should make me shiver but it doesn't. Her warmth, the look of love and desire in her beautiful light brown eyes, the way she holds me, smiles at me, moves with me - it's like I'm lost in a trance with her. My analytical mind usually wants to examine everything and know why and how something works, but tonight I just want to feel. What does this dinner, this dance mean to her? Why do I feel like the only woman in the world right now? Her soft hands smooth up and down my back as we move with the music, the wind blowing our hair around us. She stops momentarily, pulling her hair into a bun and I try (and fail) to hide my pout at losing sight of its beauty falling down her face and lightly brushing past her shoulders and neckline. She notices my pout and presses closer to me, towering over my smaller frame. With her medium stature, full breasts and adorable smile all I want is to taste her, devour her...but somehow, I manage to control myself.

This woman owns me; she can keep me forever if she wanted.

"What's wrong? Don't you like the music? Or maybe you're cold?" She runs her hands up and down my arms in an effort to warm me, but I shake my head, swaying in tandem with her.

"Let me know what I can do to make you smile," she says as I stand on my tip toes, cupping her face. Then, I undo the band from her hair, running my fingers through it as I fluff it back over her face. Her eyes close and she smiles while a gentle moan escapes from her lips.

"You're stunning with your hair down," I murmur, caressing her cheeks as our eyes are locked.

"I'll always wear it like this for you," Anna replies with a beautiful smile. The pull between us is undeniable; here I am with Anna Stonewell, in my embrace, looking as if she wants to devour me. I lick my lips as we move together still holding her face in my hands, lost in this beautiful moment that I never want to end. She leans down and brushes her forehead against mine; then I lift my head gently, nuzzling my nose against hers and our lips are just inches apart.

"Kiss me, Anna," I whisper, my heart and hazy desire taking over. She doesn't hesitate, her lips softly brushing against mine, the warmth and pleasantness of her breath inflaming my whole body. Her kiss is delicate, sweet, and almost respectful. But then the kiss gets more intense, her hands moving from my waist and arms to cradle my face as she pulls me closer and deeper into it; her tongue gliding over my lips, begging to be let in - and I allow myself to succumb to it, letting her ravish me. I moan, gasp, holding onto her tighter while trying to press our bodies together until she laughs and shuts off my irrational impulse. She falls back on the hood of the car and I press myself against her, almost as if trying to climb on top of her. My dress rides up my ass, and I can feel the cool air of the crisp fall weather as my panties are exposed.

"Damn, Elena!" She giggles. I catch my breath, stepping back from her car to look at the hood that was bearing the weight of our passionate kissing session; worrying if I have destroyed something.

"Oh shit!" I mumble, rubbing my temples with one hand. My lips still are swollen from our amorous kissing session and already I miss her against them; missing the heat of her body on mine. She stands adjusting her shirt and sweater before coming towards me again.

"Did I mess up your car? I'm so sorry!" I stammer in fright but she grabs my arm, pulling me back towards her with a grip on my breasts. She smiles, embracing me even more tightly.

"I don't care about the car, Elena." She straightens out my dress which had been riding up on my hips revealing my buttocks and underwear. "Just slow down a bit. You are mine now, Elena. I'm not going anywhere." Leaning in for another kiss we both get startled by the sudden voices of strangers coming from the park.

"Well, what do we have here?" one of them growls. The stench of marijuana hangs heavily in the air, and I spot a bottle of alcohol in one of the other men's hands. These guys are all much bigger than us. We are so screwed. Three of them, looking like typical rich college students; I've seen their faces before.

The biggest one steps forward. "Looks like our lucky night, fellas. Two lesbians just walked right into us at the park – time for us to show 'them how real men do it."

I take a step back and Anna pushes me behind her. "No, Anna," I whisper to her quietly, "let's go."

"Jack, isn't it? Yeah, I know who you are," she says with a sneer.

"Anna Stonewell, the daughter of some bigshot around here. Got yourself a little plaything? Isn't she pretty? How about you let me have a little fun with her." He grabs her arm with brute force, but Anna shows us all that she's one of the best fighters around town. With a few deft movements, she flips him over her shoulder and twists his arm while he lands up flat on his back with a thud that makes me wince – did she break something? His buddies start stepping forward to help him out, but before they can get close enough, Anna pulls out a pistol from behind her and points it their way.

"We were just trying to have an enjoyable evening," she states coolly, "but if that's not possible then I'm not opposed to adding a little bloodshed to our night."

"Chill, Anna; we were just joking around." One of Jack's friends blurts out. Anna grasps the weapon and points it towards Jack, who's screaming in pain from her grip on his arm.

"I understand, Jack. We must look like two women who can be easily pushed around."

"Anna, stop!" I plead, my entire body trembling as I stare at her in terror with the gun pointed at his temple. She doesn't even look at me; her attention seems to be focused only on her mission. Her mission right now was to inflict pain on him.

"Take me home, Anna; please take me home." I plead again, and she finally raises her eyes to meet mine. Her gaze is almost hostile, but then her face softens quickly and she steps away from Jack, releasing his hand while still holding her firearm.

Carefully, she crosses over him and helps me into the

passenger seat of the car, then walks around to the driver's side and gets in, quickly reversing out of the park before racing back into town.

"No," she says firmly, veering through the city streets away from my apartment. No? What did she mean? She'd had a gun pointed at a man - our date clearly cut short. Where is she taking me? After several twists and turns, we reach the University district - a twenty-minute bus ride away from where I live outside of campus. She pulls into a small Victorian styled house situated in the driveway and switches off the engine. This is her home. Then she looks over at me.

"No, Elena. I won't take you back to your apartment yet. I'm frustrated that our evening keeps being interrupted by inconsiderate people." Her touch is gentle, like a warm summer breeze, but the strength in her squeeze sends a jolt of electricity through my heart. After she helps me out of the car, we ascend the stairs together before she unlocks her door and steps aside for me to enter first. As I do, she follows behind me and locks the door. She then takes off her sweater and hangs it on the coat rack.

Her home is beautiful, but its contents are packed up as if she were planning a move. Furniture is wrapped in plastic sheets and boxes are everywhere, making my heart rate spike with anxiety. Is she leaving? Will I have to bid her farewell? Is she moving back home? I certainly can't lose Anna now—not after finally having a chance to be close to her.

9

———————

Anna

I'm still seething, ready to rip Jack apart and I will—later. I survey Elena, looking at the view of my home. Why does she feel sorry for those bastards? That makes me madder than anything else. I need a drink to cool down; otherwise, I'll hunt him out tonight. I think I scared him enough to make him pee in his pants. These gutless men know I'd be quicker to fire on their senselessness than another man. Because I would. Without batting an eye, I could kill them all—Jordan, that vile boss of hers, then Jack. Their heads are what I desire. But the grief-filled expression on Elena is enough to ease my rage for a moment. She looks crestfallen and glancing around my home. Leaving her alone for a bit, I step into the kitchen and grab a bottle of red wine. What I really want is something stronger, something darker, but hunger grips me instead. Because my appetite lies with Elena. Before long she follows me, stopping in the doorway looking dispirited.

"What's wrong, Elena?" My voice is demanding but gentle. "I'm not apologizing for protecting you..."

"No," she interjects. "I don't care about those scoundrels. Are you moving away?" Concern cloaks her voice like fog hovering around trees on an early morning. Strangely, I cock my head - that's what she's worried about? Me leaving her behind? Amused by her response, I laugh because it's absurd.

"Yes," I answer, taking a sip of my drink, surprised by how her face falls again. She's not losing me; she's coming with me. But I didn't know just how much Elena cares for me - it increases my yearning for her even more.

"But..." She stops, taking in a deep breath, her eyes welling with tears. She wants to cry. Over this? Why? She looks away from me, her eyes going to the floor.

"Elena," I breathe, calming myself from those assholes so I can tend to her. She needs my comfort right now.

"Are you moving back home?" I smile, though she doesn't see it. Elena is concerned about losing me - something she'll never have to worry about ever again.

"No, Elena." I respond, taking a sip of my drink - curious to know just how much this hurts for her: could I be any more of a bastard right now? Watching my sweetheart in pain yet there's a remedy for it. She gasps again and a tear escapes her, trickling down her face; my thirst for her still unslaked though. I take another sip of my drink, watching her; no food until my craving for Elena is sated. I want to taste, explore her body, and make her quiver with passion.

"Where are you moving?" She asks me with the saddest look in her beautiful olive eyes. Elena looks as if she's about to break down in tears.

"Somewhere very far from here."

"Can I use your bathroom, please?" She says, edging

away. No, she's not getting away that easily. Placing my drink down on the counter, I rush around to trap her in the hallway, pushing her against the wall. She's weeping, bawling, tears rolling down her face. I secure her wrists, preventing her from escaping me.

"Elena, why are you crying, darling?" I ask her. She avoids my gaze.

"I—I was hoping for something more from you." She stammers, still weeping. Oh yeah, I do want much more than this, but what I want would frighten her right now. I must go slow with this plan and gradually win her over. Or else I could just sedate her straight away, pack her up and take her to my father's mansion while we wait for our flight. Because we're leaving; I can't leave here without her - I won't.

"This is something more." I tell her. She looks at me, shaking her head.

"No. I was hoping this was more than a fling, a one-time thing. I want to see you every day, be with you. Even if I have work and school, I can still make time for us." She looks at me pleadingly, entirely unaware of my intentions. Her words ring out now, but will she feel the same when I take her to meet my father? Or when we wed tomorrow, will she come willingly or kicking and screaming? I move my hands from her wrists and tenderly caress her cheeks before softly kissing her. She responds eagerly, drawing me closer to her.

"You can't leave me," she breathes against my lips. "I just got you." A small smile spreads on my lips as I kiss her again. Will she fight for me?

"Elena, stop." I say quietly, despite feeling an ache in my gut as she takes my hand between our bodies, pushing it up further until my fingers are met with the wetness of her panties. Ahh...she's playing dirty now.

"I want you, Anna. Please," Her voice is barely audible, muffled by our kisses as she pushes herself into my fingers and moans into them.

"Elena..." I exhale in surprise at her advances. With every touch and every kiss, I can feel how much she wants me; the way her fingertips tug at my hair intensifies with each passing second.

"I want you Anna - I want you inside me." My face stretches into a satisfied grin as her words escape her lips and cannot be taken back. *She wants me?* I'm curious to discover where this conversation will lead us both next...Is it the wine? Has it made her more open?

"What will you do to keep me, Elena?" My fingers curl around the fabric of her panties as I sink two digits deep inside her and she gasps, pressing her body against the wall. I yearn to take her upstairs and consummate this desire, but not before I obtain an answer from her.

"Anything." She breathes, undulating in time with my thrusts, cupping my face and ensnaring me in a passionate kiss. With one hand, I massage her insides while the other pulls down on the fabric of her dress until her ample breasts are freed for me to adore.

"Elena, what will you do to keep me? Will you follow me?" She shudders from pleasure as my hands work their magic upon her body.

"Would you leave with me, Elena? Would you follow me wherever I go?"

"Ah!" She screams out, her walls squeezing my digits tightly as she reaches a powerful climax against me.

"Yes!" she screams, and that's all I need to hear. Time to take this to the bedroom, where I plan to break her in half, ravish her sweet pussy and make her bend to my whim. Drawing out my fingers from her, I drop them into my mouth, relishing in the taste of her blissful climax. Closing my eyes, I let the craze, the darkness inside me take over. As of now, Anna is gone, and the creature, the murkiness hidden deep in me is primed, ruling over me. I've attempted to restrain myself for so long, shielding Anna from my obscurity, maintaining a distance with her as much as possible, but I can't any longer. After getting a taste of her, feeling her body close to mine, feeling her love. I can't restrain myself any more. She's mine. Mine always and forever. Seizing the back of her neck harshly, I push her up the stairs to my nearly vacant bedroom which only holds a bed and dresser; the rest of the room is filled with boxes. Throwing her down roughly onto the bed, she lands on her face and stomach. She raises herself up, wriggling on the bed eyeing me with an appalled expression. Even she can see it: Anna is gone, someone else lives within me now -the beast that hungers for her being, wishes to devour each inch of her including her spirit.

"Anna?" she murmurs, clearly unsure of who is here now. Not taking my eyes away from hers, I start to undress myself and soon stand before her completely naked. She attempts to flee as I move closer to the bed - yet I catch hold of her ankle before she can escape, dragging her back towards me. She yelps and struggles, her dress riding up her ass - exposing her jet-black silk panties. I flip her over and straddle her body on the mattress.

"Anna!" she screams fearfully as our entwined bodies become one. Placing a hand on each side of her face, I passionately connect our mouths in an electrifying kiss. Can she feel it? Can she feel my endless devotion for the past year? Ravishingly biting down on her lip, I pour out all my love into her, our bond becoming more overwhelming with every passing second. Gazing deep into my eyes, she watches in awe as tears stream down my face - wishing for Elena to see everything about me; from the passionate lover to the cold-hearted monster that will take everything but feel nothing for it. Though there is no remorse for what's about to happen - only desire, love and need for Elena.

I crave her.

"Anna don't cry. I'm yours, all of me," she says softly while stroking my face. I already know that; she has always been mine. But it's pleasing to hear her say it again. We lock eyes for an extended moment before she whispers the words that I have longed to hear, words only spoken once before—the first night I snuck into her apartment when she was asleep.

"I love you, Anna," she whispers, and then all restraint vanishes as a flurry of emotion sweeps over me.

10

───────

Elena

"I love you, Anna." The words escape me, my emotions overwhelming me. I shouldn't have said that. She doesn't know me, and Anna owes me nothing - is this an attempt of manipulation to keep her with me? Desperation is evident; no denying or hiding that. But the words that escaped me are true. I love her. I've loved her for some time now, unable to show her nor tell her how I really felt; only watch from a distance. Until now we're here – in each other's embrace, holding one another, loving each other. Anna stares at me, listening to my words. It's okay if she doesn't feel the same; I've accepted her rejection of my feelings for her. I'm okay with it. Anna tenderly cups my face, gazing into my eyes overflowing with affection. My heart swells. She's in the nude atop me, her beautiful plump breasts pressing against my chest.

"Elena, my plans... I—I need to tell you something." I hush her, placing a finger to her lips, shaking my head, tears welling in my eyes. No. Please don't ruin this wondrous moment - let me feel your love. She's leaving soon by the way she's packed up, likely tomorrow.

No...

"I love you, Anna." I whisper it again, needing her to understand the depths of my emotions. I want her to know that my heart belongs entirely to her, and if she desires, she can keep it with her forever. I may suffer, but at least she'll have something of mine. I love her more than anything in this world.

"Elena," she groans, exhaling a heavy sigh, and presses her lips to mine. This kiss is full of love and passion that leaves me breathless; I wrap my arms around her, pushing my legs wide apart. She grinds into me, the heat from my core radiating against her. It's as if she has no control over her body, kissing me hungrily and roaming her hands all over me. She hurriedly rips my dress off, the thin fabric tearing under her strong grasp. She tugs hard on my panties until they rip away and hit the floor. Her fingers quickly slide between my thighs, massaging my slick folds and teasing me.

"You're mine, Elena. You'll be mine forever. I'm keeping you, honey. Where I go, you will go. You'll remain with me forever. I will do anything to keep you. I'll even die for you, Elena. And kill for you if need be. But you're mine and don't forget it. Say it." She slides two fingers inside me and I cling tightly to her body as I'm ready to climax again. Yes, yes, I am hers. I must find a way to make it work between us even though it is long-distance. There are many successful relationships like that in this world; maybe I can convince her to stay a little longer so that I can move closer to her? Though ditching school would not be an option as it is my only chance of escaping poverty; I cannot depend on Anna too much either; instead, I must prove myself and show the world that I can take care of me. As she strongly fucks me, thrusting her fingers in and out of me repeatedly, all the while aggressively dominating me, forcing me into submission - making me solely hers - I bite hard on her neck, moaning with pleasure as my body rocks against hers desperately.

"You're mine, Elena. Say it!" Ah fuck! I come hard, screaming as I writhe against her.

"Yes! I'm yours!" With my proclamation, she bows her head between my legs, filling me with pleasure. Without a moment spared, she sweeps her tongue along the folds of my pussy - brushing, licking, sucking. She's relentless in her pursuit to drive me wild. Her touch is electric; she seems to know all the right places to caress me and the precise angles to move within me to make me shatter into pieces.

Her hand moves up to my breast, slapping, gripping, teasing my nipples. I put my hands over my head, thrashing from side to side trying to fight against the passion, but no; Anna is shattering me. I come again, hard, screaming wanting to break in half. She sits up flipping me over onto my stomach gripping my hips and pulling my ass back to her. I push my body up onto the bed resting on my hands and knees looking back at her wondering what she's about to do. She pulls me back into her grinding into my ass and I can feel her clit brushing against me. She moans backing me into her again and again grinding into me, fucking me. I aid her by backing my ass into her forming a wicked grin against my face proud that I can get her off. I want her to come hard so I can lick every inch of her; fuck her, taste her, drink her dry. Wiggling my ass as she grinds into me smiling and looking back at her dripping with sweat eyes shut, head tilted back enjoying the roundness of my ass smacking my flesh grinding into me, coming hard against my skin.

Her hands dig into my waist, and she grinds into me one final time, whimpering, cursing, smacking my ass again as she collapses to the side. I seize the moment of her vulnerability and clamber atop her, pressing our bare skin together in a feverish embrace. I feel the pulsing thud of her heart against mine. She averts her gaze away from me, gazing up at the ceiling.

I lower my head between her legs, spreading them wide for me and burying my face in her slick folds. She cries out my name in surprise as her hands slam down onto the sheets and she lifts her face to watch me as I savor her orgasmic pleasure.

"Elena! Ah, fuck!" she yells. But it doesn't matter; I want more of her taste to linger on my tongue. And I want this to be something more than a mere fling. It has to be special. I'll do whatever it takes to make that happen—fuck her into oblivion if necessary. Anna is my saving grace in this harsh world: she offered me an opportunity, and I'm sure as hell taking it. With one last primal grind against my lips, I bury myself further into her pussy pushing my tongue inside of her as far as it will go.

"Come on my face, Anna." I command. My words send a jolt through her body, causing her to grind into me again. Screams escape her lips as the pleasure of my orgasm takes over. Instantly, she grips a lock of my hair and with sheer strength lifts me up onto her. Sitting up with me still in her arms, our lips connect in a passionate kiss with the taste of our climaxes mingling between one another. The love I feel for this woman is like nothing else and it's devastating to think I might lose her.

"No, don't cry Elena; just feel, baby." Reassuringly, Anna kisses me and tenderly runs her hands along my back. "I love you, Elena. I love you so much, baby." Her declaration of love takes my breath away; nothing else matters right now but her love and I want to feel only that.

"I love you, Elena; this is forever," she declares as she lays me gently down on my back before climbing on top of me and making sweet, passionate love to me. My insatiable pussy craves satisfaction every day if possible; can Anna handle it? This is the most beautiful and intense experience of my life; I will take it with me to the grave.

11

———————

Anna

Here I lie in bed, unable to sleep, watching Elena's chest rise and fall as she soothes off to sleep. I take a deep breath, chuckling at how insatiable this woman truly is. Oh my god, that was an insane night of sex. Elena let me fuck her the way I wanted and feel her the way I had always dreamed of feeling her. Usually, I got chastised for the way I enjoyed fucking, the positions I loved to move in, but with Elena everything is different; like she actually enjoys my favorite positions too. She rests on her stomach with her hair sprawled messily across her face and hands tucked under her pillow. I fight the urge to climb on top and do it all over again, last night was unbelievable, everything I ever wished for. There's no getting past this; I'm addicted to Elena now. She is now the only woman that can satisfy me. She owns me. Sitting up on the bed, I reach down to grab my phone from my pants pocket and dial the special security team my father has hired to watch over me throughout this entire process.

"Pack up her apartment. I want it to look like she's moved out." I end the call, completing the last steps of my scheme. Then I open the drawer, taking out the syringe and sedation medicine that my brother Aberto gave me before he left. He too will be dragging his beloved wife along - whether she wants it or not. This is and will be the toughest component of the plan. Getting Elena to understand she has no option. She belongs to me, body, and soul. We can't endure another day apart. Much like my mother did with my father, Elena will come around eventually. I just need to ready myself for how long until she confides in me again. I can't rest. I'll have no peace until we are on the plane, traveling to our secluded island, where we'll spend the remainder of our lives, only flying to the mainland for food and provisions.

I'm ready for this. I've spent my entire life preparing for this moment, and luckily my sweet Elena rests beside me in bed. She whispered her love for me earlier, and I'll give her the world in return for her heart. As she shifts, I move closer to her, wrapping my arms around her bare body and pressing myself against hers. She smiles lightly, filled with pleasure and comfort.

"Mmmn, Anna," she moans as I kiss her neck and inhale her scent. But soon, Elena will be feeling emotions far different from the ones we're feeling now. Hatred and disgust may be among them once reality sets in. I'll do anything for Elena, including granting Elena's every desire - except leaving me. It's not going to be easy on poor Elena when I take away everything she's worked so hard for during her years of study. However, it's doubtful that anyone will miss Elena once she's gone. Even her mother can't care less if she only shows up during the holidays, and she has no friends here except the elderly neighbor whom I intend to look after. There isn't even another person in town that Elena has loved before me. Did I choose her for this reason - because I knew that there would never be anyone else to come between us?

I realize how far I had gone when I first broke into her apartment, pulling up a chair and brushing my fingers through her hair. That was going to be my last night breaking in—I knew I had taken it too far. Buying the building she lived in so I could gain unlimited access wasn't enough. Then there was Ms. Laura, Elena's elderly friend who saw me coming in daily. But it all came together that one fateful night of my stalking when Elena sighed heavily, turning on her side in sleep, murmuring my name and admitting that she loved me. I can still hear the echo of her voice that night when she told me she loved me.

Yes, she was in a deep slumber and possibly dreaming, but even in Elena's dreams, she loves me. I felt my entire body harden that night, and Elena became the object of my desires. I wanted nothing else in that moment. Only, Elena.

I'd heard those words uttered to me many times—especially by Alexa and Samantha—but I never felt compelled to reciprocate until Elena entered my life. The emotions she stirs in me are beyond explanation; all I'm aware of is how agonizing the thought of losing her is. I've attempted to conduct myself properly for her, tried to keep her away from my insanity, yet still, I couldn't resist drawing closer to her. She writhes against me, rubbing her luscious ass against my vulva as I restrain myself from grinding into her. I want her wide awake when I ravage her again. Nestling my face in her throat, I grip onto her tightly, inhaling slowly and closing my eyes as sleep overwhelms me, knowing that soon enough I'll need to fight with her. Elena will attempt to flee, battle with me, yell for assistance—but she won't be able to escape me. Because she doesn't know how it was all pre-decided: planned to keep her; planned to always remain together; planned to adore her forever. She's the love of my life, more valuable than anything else in this world. Inhaling her aroma is like a narcotic—and after finally feeling secure and contented, slumber overtakes me.

12

Elena

My eyes flutter open to the sounds of boxes and equipment being moved around. I sit up, sheet clutched to my bare chest, rubbing my eyes while surveying the nearly empty room; all of the boxes are gone, except for a dresser and the bed I am resting on. The thought that movers have been in here as I lay asleep sends a shiver down my spine. Running a hand over my face, I remember the night of passion with Anna, how she ripped away all of my clothes. What will I wear? Wrapping the sheet tightly around me, I walk over to the dresser but find clothes already laid out on the bed - a tank top and sweatpants along with a bra and panties that look as if they fit perfectly. Hurrying to the master bathroom, there's a brand-new toothbrush awaiting me along with other items. After brushing my teeth and washing my face, I grab the towel and washcloth provided and hop in the shower, giving myself a quick scrub before applying deodorant and sliding into the clothes; surprisingly, they are an ideal fit and so comfortable.

My spirits sink as I hear the movers continuing to haul boxes and furniture out of the house. Does she have to move right now? My night of pleading seems to have done nothing. She still wants to go. Does she want me to leave too? Why does my heart feel like it's going to burst just at the thought? I love her. Anna, I love her so much. There has to be a way I can persuade her to give this a chance. Last night was so special. We can make a long-distance relationship work. I tie my hair into a bun, take in a deep breath, then start walking down the stairs, watching as the movers take the last of her furniture out of the living room. After scouring the main floor, I find her in the kitchen making breakfast with surprising effort. She's wearing an apron and dishing out eggs onto two plates that already feature fruit, biscuits, and bacon. Beside them stand two tall glasses of orange juice. And Anna looks beautiful. Her gorgeous hair is pulled into a ponytail, emphasizing her tattoos, and she's wearing a tank top and sweatpants. When she notices me step in, she smiles warmly.

"Good morning, sweetheart. Did you sleep well?" I walk over to the counter and stare down at the food, not answering her. I don't know why I'm acting like this. Last night was amazing, but she doesn't owe me anything. And look how quickly I have regressed into Alex and Samantha's mindset—begging her for another chance.

"Don't be that way, sweetheart. Didn't you enjoy yourself last night?" I look up at her and frown.

"You're still leaving." Unable to stop the pout forming on my face. Oh, my freaking god, what is wrong with me? Anna smiles, placing the pan in the sink before walking over and pulling me into her arms. The sweet tropical fruit scent envelopes me as she holds me tightly.

"Yes, Elena. I am moving. As much as I'd like to stay, I can't—this is a family obligation. But don't worry—you're coming with me. She kisses me lightly on the forehead before grabbing the plates and setting them down on the table then retrieving the orange juice. Once the table is set for breakfast, she pulls out a chair for me to sit in. Meanwhile, I'm flabbergasted—not understanding what she means when she says that 'I'm coming with her.' How could this be possible? I have school; it's already bad enough that I'll miss today's classes because of our date last night! This scholarship is a once-in-a-lifetime opportunity; I can't let this slip away from my grasp.

"Come, join me for breakfast, sweetheart." Taking a deep breath, I sit down beside her. I have to let her down gently; I can't compromise on school, but I want this to work. There has to be a way. She smiles, watching me as I gulp my orange juice and take a bite of bacon.

"I can't come with you." I say once I'd finish chewing my food. "I'm in school on a scholarship. If I screw this up, it's back to Brookside for me—somewhere I never want to see again." Anna digs into her food, seemingly ignoring me. What didn't she understand?

"There's online college now; money isn't something you have to worry about with me around, Elena. I'll take care of it all for you." I groan inwardly. She is so privileged, so wealthy—able to get whatever she wanted whenever she wanted it. You can't just ask me to drop out of school; no matter how much love there is between us, we need to be realistic here.

"Anna...I can't do that." My heart beaks as the words

leave my lips. Why did she need to move anyway? She's almost finished with college—all she needs are a few extra courses and an economics class; what was the big deal? Anna finishes her breakfast, then her warm beautiful face suddenly shifts into a cold, menacing glare that almost makes me recoil when our eyes meet again.

"You can, Elena. And you will. It won't be easy for you, but I'll be here each step of the way."

I put my fork down, staring at her with confusion. What is she talking about?

"Ms. Stonewell, we are finished and the apartment on North Avenue is ready too. Anything else you'd like us to do?" The mover asks from the doorway of the kitchen. Apartment on North Avenue? That's my street. Does Anna have an apartment there too? She smiles at me, then stands from the table and hands him a generous tip.

"Thanks a lot Ms. Stonewell!" He says quickly before hurrying away as if he's afraid Anna will change her mind about such a generous tip.

"You have an apartment on North Avenue too?" I question her nervously as goosebumps scatter across my arms. She shakes her head in reply.

"Who are you moving out then?" I ask gulping back the uneasiness that start to rise within me.

"You, honey. I told you - I'm moving and you're coming with me." My heart drops into my stomach as shock floods my body. Did she really just pack up my apartment while I slept after one date and one night of sex? Please tell me if this is a joke!

"You're kidding right?" I laugh nervously, but her serious expression leaves no room for doubt - she isn't joking around. What did she do with all of my things?

"I insist that you put everything back this instant. You don't have the authority to pack up my apartment, Anna. What in the world are you thinking?" Her words are as still as her demeanor. She reclines in her chair, pulling her orange juice closer to her lips.

"I'm in love, Elena. I've loved you for a while now." My footsteps feel heavy as I slowly step away from her; she doesn't spare me a glance, only continuing to focus on her meal.

"I anticipated that this would not be easy for you, Elena. But regardless of your feelings on the matter, I have made a decision. You will come with me, my sweetheart." Her words are coated in honey, but I can see the venom lurking beneath the surface. The urge to flee from her grasp wells up within me, and I shake my head vigorously as I back away. She has no right to dictate what I do or where I go. My instincts scream at me to escape, to run far away from this woman who now poses a threat to my existence. Without looking back, I sprint towards the front door, heart pounding in my chest. My feet padded against the hardwood floors, but then a towering figure standing like a wall between me and freedom. My momentum carries me straight into his arms. He lifts me off the ground and carries me back into the house. The sound of the door slamming shut behind us echoes through my thoughts as the world around me disappears into darkness.

A hulking figure strides in seconds after the door slams, with a syringe clutched in his hand. I'm doomed. Panic rises as the door slams shut behind him and he moves to my side. The giant shackles my arms while he stabs a needle into my arm and swiftly removes it. He drops me like a sack of dirt and I tumble to the ground, eyes darting back to Anna standing at the kitchen doorway with her hands buried deep in her pockets, watching the horror unfold. No! This is really happening. I'm being kidnapped. Pushing off with my elbows, I scuttle backwards, quickly rolling onto my hands and feet before taking off like lightning from the two men. But Anna steps out of the kitchen doorway just in time to catch me around my waist and hoist me up, my feet dangling in the air.

"Oh, sweetheart, don't fight this. I'm offering you a new life—a better one. You won't experience any more suffering or struggling." Her words make it to my ears, but they are difficult to comprehend. My body is in survival mode, I must free myself from her. I use my elbow and thrust it into her chest. She gasps and winces, releasing me. Before the men can grab me, I start running up the stairs with only the smaller man catching onto my ankle. But I manage to stop him by lashing out with the back of my foot into his face before sprinting upstairs to the bedroom. In that moment, I spot my purse laying atop the dresser; I snatch it up and bolt into the bathroom, locking the door behind me. The man begins pounding at it and kicking it as well, making me thankful for these strong Victorian doors; they're sturdy enough to hold him off temporarily. Quickly ransacking my purse on the tiled floor in search of my phone, darkness starts to consume me. 'I need to call the police', I think but can barely make out anything due to the blurring vision and my weakening body. By using the counter of the sink as support, I attempt to lift myself off the floor but flop back down weakly onto my bottom instead. Exhaustion is all that remains.

My eyelids grow heavy, the last thought I remember being the realization that they had drugged me. My head slams onto the unforgiving tile floor as the door kicks open.

Through my blurry vision, I see Anna rushing to my side. She tenderly lifts my head into her lap, stroking my cheek with a comforting touch.

"It's ok," she whispers softly, just before everything goes dark.

13

Anna

Iknew this wouldn't be easy. Everywhere I looked, the writing on the wall was clear. Though, I hadn't expected Elena to be such a fighter; it only fanned the flames of my desire for her more. Julian, one of my security guards, steps forward as I hold Elena in my arms – waiting for my command. She lies peacefully, her breathing deep and even. I check her pulse again to make sure she is alright. I don't want to let her go, but if I want her safely at my father's mansion then I have to.

"Madam Stonewell," he says cautiously as he kneels down and carefully scoops her from my arms. I scowl at him; addressing me like that was his instructions from my father, but damnit I can't stand it. Seeing Elena in this state bothers me deeply. It had to be done though, otherwise she would've screamed all the way to the car. A tear wells in my eye and I nod, allowing Julian to take my sweetheart away from me. Her mouth parts slightly while breathing steadily as he lifts her away from me. Enzo steps aside, his bulky frame blocking the doorway as Julian carries Elena out of the room.

"Secure her well, just in case she regains consciousness." Enzo's request to Julian reminds me that they are professionals at this line of work and that I can trust them with my life. Enzo's head almost touches the ceiling of the bathroom as he reached out his hand for me. Taking it, he helps me back onto my feet and places his hand against my shoulder.

"Anna." I fixate him with a cold stare before he can call me by some formal title. He shrugs in response, rolling his eyes before speaking again.

"Believe me; if there was a better way, I would have taken it. If you prefer, you can escort her where she needs to go, but it will have to be like this." I give a nod and he steps aside from the doorframe, allowing me to pass through. Once outside, Enzo slides open the inside pocket of his coat and hands me a pistol, checking for bullets before handing it over.

"You said you wanted to make a stop before we go back to your father?" He reminds me, raising an eyebrow. If there's anything Enzo loves, it's a hit. But this isn't the typical one: I'm putting these men out of their misery. No more tormenting women, especially that bastard Jordan. As soon as Elena's gone, he'll just find another poor innocent girl to attack.

Enzo adjusts his coat, rubbing a hand over his sweaty forehead; as a large-framed man, he's seemingly always perspiring. He gives me a nod and I place the gun in the back of my pants, then grab my jacket from the closet, slipping it on before putting on some sneakers. No need to wash the dishes - the clean-up crew will take care of the rest. I grab my wallet and toss it to Enzo, as he'll need to burn it. The minute our flight takes off, I'm no longer Anna Stonewell; Anna Stonewell will be dead to everyone in this town.

"How long will she be out?" I ask him. I need to know; I want to be there when she wakes up so she has a familiar face in her sight.

"Two or three hours, tops." I give him a nod and lead the way out of the room, eager to take care of some unfinished business with Jordan and Jack - I'm not leaving without a little blood on my hands.

I'm a monster, born and raised by Antonio Stonewell. He harbored me along with my two brothers in darkness. Vengeance is best served cold and bloody, so I won't leave until their heads are on stakes. But I must be swift; I want Elena to be safe in my arms when she wakes. She's my everything; the last thing I want is for her to experience more terror than what she's already feeling, particularly under the watch of my father and two brothers—the monsters that formed me into what I am today. It would be likely they'll put her up with the other ladies who are confined to a room as we wait for our get away.

Elena isn't a prisoner, she's my wife. I need to make her understand that with time, she'll come around and love me in the way that I desperately crave. I've longed for Elena for months, wishing to experience her body as I did last night. And oh, my God - she exceeded my expectations. Our first night of love making wasn't awkward like I'd feared; instead, it was as if we were destined to be together. Elena knows how to fuck, and she does it well. On the outside, she may seem like a sweetheart - a bookworm who cares about her studies- but underneath is something special... a dark side to her passions. I had an inkling of this from watching her sleep over the past six months and from noticing her need to masturbate before going to bed. But her moves in the actual act of sex shocked me. Her whispers of love sealed her fate with me: I'm never letting Elena go. Never. She'll stay mine until I take my last breath, and even then, I'll find a way to keep her with me in the afterlife.

14

______

Elena

My eyes flutter open upon Anna, my head resting in her lap and my head aching. Was I dreaming? Did I hit my head or something? Then, the events leading to my sudden slumber come back to me and I widen my eyes, quickly noticing that my hands are bound together by a thick rope. Anna's gentle touches brush over my shoulder and I flinch from the pain radiating from the back of my head; however, I can't reach it. Scanning around the room nervously, I take in my surroundings. I'm in a study with bookcases lining the walls, and on a long leather couch.

"Elena, it's alright, sweetheart." Anna tries to console me, but I shift my body away from her, attempting to move my legs only to discover they are bound as well. I bring my restrained legs to the floor, aligning myself away from Anna on the couch, and assuming a sitting position. My gaze roams around the room once more and I notice an older man in one of the lounge chairs with a lit cigar in hand while smoke escapes his mouth. His features resemble Anna's—this must be her father. Despite being aware of the Stonewell's notorious wealth and influence in Traverse City, I refrain from screaming realizing that all her father needs is a wave of his hand for the men who drugged me to silence me. As Anna moves closer on the sofa, she softly strokes my cheek while pushing back some loose strands of hair. She hushes me in a whisper, muttering soothing words into my ear.

"It's alright, darling. You're protected here, with me." I stare at her incredulously as if she has gone mad. Of course, I'm not going anywhere when my hands and feet are tied—I'm a prisoner here.

"Anna, let me go home," I beg her yet she continues stroking my cheek without taking any notice of me.

"So, this is the woman you want to spend your whole life with?" Her father's words are laced with sarcasm and then he gives a wave of his hand to a man dressed in a butler's uniform. The employee nods, then goes to the bar and pours a drink for Anna's father. She averts her gaze from me as she glares at him. "No, father, don't." She snaps at him. He emits an audible huff and takes a swig of his beverage, disregarding her protest, but refraining from further provocation.

"Anna, what's going on? I don't get it."

"Just make sure she keeps it down," he orders coldly, "or otherwise I'll have Julian and Enzo take her upstairs with the others. I'm not in the mood to hear her complaints." Her glare intensifies as my tears swell with fear and outrage. Why would she do this? Why won't she let me go?

"We discussed this last night, sweetheart. You said you loved me and I reciprocated," a pleading tone resonates in her voice.

"Do you honestly think I'd leave you now that I know

how you feel about me?" Oh, God! This woman is insane! I struggle futilely to move away from her as she presses closer every time I try to scoot away. Finally, she leans in and kisses my cheek.

"Why am I tied up?" Her father's laughter echoes throughout the room, and Anna groans as she softly kisses my cheek. The sweatpants and tank top she wore earlier have been replaced with her signature gear—tight ripped jeans and a fitted t-shirt. Her hair is down, cascading swiftly over her face in waves—just the way I love it. She's wearing light makeup on her eyes and lashes. She looks stunning.

"Because you'll run. And I've got something special planned for us tonight; I can't have you running away. Julian and Enzo will have to put you to sleep again," she says.

"Anna," I plead, tears dripping down my face. "You can't keep me like this; you have to let me go." But she doesn't even acknowledge me. Instead, she turns to the two men—Julian and Enzo—and gives them a subtle nod.

Anna turns to her men and barks out orders. "Take her upstairs for me, please. I'd like to get her ready for our wedding." The words hit me like a punch in the gut. Wedding? What the fuck is going on here? Panic set in as the two men approach me and lift me up effortlessly, despite my struggles. Anna trails behind us with an affectionate smile on her face.

As we make our way through the opulent mansion, my thoughts race. Were Samantha and Alexa aware of how fucking psycho this family is? How could I have been so stupid as to get myself involved with them?

I try to stay calm and think rationally as we ascend the grand staircase and are led down a long hallway to a set of double doors. My heart pounded in my chest as one of the men kick open the doors and toss me onto a massive bed.

Trembling, I look up at him as he pulls out a large blade from his suit jacket and holds it out to me.

"I'm gonna cut you loose, Elena. You better behave. Clean yourself up and change into the lovely dress Anna bought for you. If you fight, scream, or try to run away, you will be attending this wedding ceremony unconscious. Do you understand me?" I gulp nervously, nodding my head a bit too vigorously. He takes the blade to my feet first, cutting the ropes, then moving on to my wrists and setting me free. But his words still ring in my ears. I don't move an inch out of fear.

"I'll be right outside this door. Behave yourself. Be good to Anna, she loves you." He gives me a wink before leaving me alone in the room with Anna who stands by the door as soon as it's closed, watching me intently. I sit up on the bed and run a hand through my wild hair, searching for an escape route; but if I run, they'll drug me and I don't want to black out again.

"Are you hungry? You've been out a few hours now." She cracks open the door and whispers something to whoever's outside before shutting it quickly with a turn back towards me.

"Alrighty then, let me show you your dress!" Her voice is almost giddy-like and her hands are clasped together tightly. She strides over to the closet quickly, opening it up and pulling out a beautiful all black gown which she holds out to me.

"I took your measurements months ago when I spotted this dress. It's perfect for you." She says, smiling wide while extending the gown. The dress is stunning; it's completely black, tied up in a crisscross pattern, and has an open back with a mermaid hem that trails down to the floor. It seems as though the dress was made specifically to fit my body.

Suddenly, I am paralyzed. How could she have planned this out for all these months? And how did she get my measurements?

"So, you are planning on marrying me?" My voice trembles nervously. She nods vigorously, her face lights up with a proud grin.

"Yes, Elena. When I laid eyes on you for the first time, I knew that you were meant to be mine forever. I already have a similar dress in my wardrobe and thought it would be wonderful if we matched. I know you are fond of the color blue, but I was hoping you'd wear black for our wedding. So?"

"Do I have any say in the matter?" Panic rushes through me. How can she just assume that I want to get married? Anna stares at me blankly for a moment before shrugging and hanging the dress up on a hook next to the bed.

"Elena, do you not want to marry me?" Her words hang heavy in the air and I find myself unable to answer her. Although every fiber of my being screams "No" at the top of my lungs, my mouth remains silent. What is wrong with me? Why can't I speak up? Anna simply smiles at my lack of response and comes closer towards me until our faces are mere inches apart.

"I love you, Elena. I've loved you for a very long time." My heart stops as her words sink in, and I try to understand how it's possible. She's given me meager glances and small smiles all year, yet she loves me? Tears stream down my face; my body in shock. She moves closer, pressing her lips against mine. I don't pull away. The warmth of her lips, the sweetness of her breath... I'm caught under her love spell, wanting more of her taste. She's so gentle with me, even in this insanity.

"How?" I breathe between our lips. "You ignored me for the past year until last night. I don't understand, Anna."

She sighs and sits beside me, taking my hand in hers and pulling it to her lips to kiss the back of it.

"I ignored you to spare you. But I've always loved you and never wavered from how I feel about you."

"Spared me from what? Why are you kidnapping me? Why can't we just date like normal people and get to know each other?" She sighs again, keeping my hand close to her lips. Even though confusion is running through my veins, I don't withdraw my hand or be harsh with her; I just want to understand what's happening.

"My family has a tedious and ominous history. Since my great grandfather and his beloved wife first arrived here, they have lived a life of crime. We have hunted for a way out from this life - for the last few decades. My father accomplished that mission. We are leaving this place for good and fading away into oblivion." I take in a deep breath. I heard rumors about the Stonewells, their gory past, but I could never accept tales without evidence. I abhor any gossip, hating it from the core of my heart.

"So, those rumors around town...they were true after all? You're collaborating with the mafia?" She shakes her head in response to my query.

"I have no ties with whatever my father does or did, other than being his daughter."

"But you nearly killed Jack." She gulps down, avoiding eye contact with me.

"He was going to hurt you; I would do anything to protect you!" She gives me an intense look before continuing "Let me be frank with you, Elena: What do you think college will get you? A job which hardly covers your rent and debt piling on? College is just a hoax Elena; no success can be achieved through it anymore. Your aspirations will lead you to more debt than success -"

"Fuck you, Anna! That was such a low move to pull! You think you can talk down to me like this?!!" I yell at her furiously as she stands to tower over me and closes her eyes as she folds her arms.

"I apologize for being so crude, Elena. It was wrong of me."

"I don't give a damn about your opinion of my dreams! You're no different than my crappy family, making me feel the same! Fuck off and let me go home!" She casts her gaze down at me gently but looks hurt.

"My words may have been harsh, Elena. But they aren't wrong." I glance away, seething with anger. How can she be right? It's well-known that getting a great job nowadays is almost impossible - even with a degree - yet I still hold onto hope that I can beat the odds. And fuck her for bringing that up to me.

Still upset, I make a decision to turn the tables on her.

"What about you then, Anna? You've been hung up over some poor girl from Brookside. Your father was right; you deserve better than me! Why settle?" Oh shit, the way her face falls into an intense frown. Her stunning eyes were smoldering with rage. I'm in deep trouble now.

15

———

Anna

"I can't say I don't deserve this," I seethe, fuming. Did she really just say that? Do better than Elena? There's no one better. My rage boils and I instinctively grab her face, squeezing her cheeks so hard that she cries out in pain as her eyes widen.

"Don't you ever speak to me like that again. Understand?" She gulps, trembling, and nods quickly. I release her, pacing the room as my fury builds.

"You are not just some poor girl from Brookside," I snarl, stalking back and forth. "You're everything to me."

"But it's true, Anna," she chokes through her tears.

"Just like your words ring true to me. You're not wrong. I'm chasing after a dream that may be too far for me to reach —just like how you fell in love with a poor girl unworthy of your love."

I scream in frustration—and then I lose control. I pounce on her, trapping her wrists above her head and straddling her body as she gasps in fear, sobbing beneath me. Her entire body trembles with terror—but my rage won't die down easily. Elena is everything to me—and it makes me furious to see her putting herself down like this.

My heart pours out to Elena. "I will never apologize for loving you," I declare, my voice trembling with emotion.

"Last night was beautiful, Elena. You touched me in ways that I have never been touched before. I cannot forget the way you whispered sweet nothings into my ear, showering me with your love. But tell me Elena, did it mean nothing to you?" She meets my gaze momentarily but looks away without answering.

Nonetheless, I am content to endure her silence. Whatever happens, I will not let her devalue herself. She is more precious to me than gold - I will live and die for her.

"I recognize why you are angry with me," I tell her, gently leaning forward and brushing my lips against her tear-streaked cheek as my hands caress her neck. Her body responds to my touch, her breathing becoming labored.

"I need you, Elena; everything in life seems incomplete without you by my side," I continue fervently, growing more impassioned with every passing moment. "You know me - I've always planned on winning your heart slowly and steadily over time through courtship and romance... but things have changed now..."

Pausing to take in a deep breath, I glance at her with remorseful eyes.

"I can't stay here any longer Elena... If I do then I'll surely be killed..."

Her expression turns mournful and she whispers softly:

"I don't want to lose you."

"Then come away with me, my love," I implore her urgently.

"If you won't then... Well, then there is nothing left for us here together..."

She buries her head in her hands and groans – a painful sound that breaks my heart into a million pieces.

"It's not fair, Anna. You can't do this to me!" She screams out as I climb away from her. Oh, but I can – and I will. I'll take the most unlikely route if it means keeping her in my life. I love her; I need her. And she will be mine.

Just then, Enzo taps lightly on the door before entering with a tray of food with cold cut sandwiches, chips and drinks held in his hands. Elena's eyes light up at the sight of the pitcher of water and she licks her lips in anticipation. She's likely dehydrated due to the drugs she had been given recently – not to mention all the crying she has done since then.

I walk over to the cart and pour her a glass of water which I hand over to her. Hesitant at first, Elena soon gives into temptation and snatches it from me, almost gulping it down in one go. When finished, she lets out a deep breath and looks up at me, handing me back the empty cup and wiping off her mouth.

"You'll eat first," I instruct firmly while gesturing towards the plate of food on the table. "Then you'll get ready for your wedding ceremony; the officiant is arriving soon. Make sure you look presentable." Taking another step closer to her, I lock eyes with her so that there's no mistake about my words – I want compliance from her end. "Don't even think about refusing to marry me; you don't have a choice anymore. It's either you put on your dress and we stand together in front of everyone...or else you stay here while watching me die," I growl out menacingly.

Elena glares daggers at me, likely wanting nothing more than to rip my head off right at this moment. Letting out a small smirk, I step away from her while provoking another thought in my mind – how passionate our wedding night will be tonight given all the built-up anger between us. I'd love for Elena to angry fuck me.

Elena stands unsteadily, and I rush to her side, steadying her with one arm around her waist. She's far too weak for such activity, but she needs to get her bearings. I help her walk over to the tray on the bedside table and pick up a turkey sandwich. It isn't my ideal meal choice for her, she needs something warm and nourishing, but we're in a time crunch, and my father's kitchen staff have whipped up something quick for us. Elena doesn't hesitate—she devours a few turkey sandwiches along with some soda cans, rapidly eating until her hunger is sated. Once she's finished, Enzo takes the cart out of the room and closes the door behind him. I take her into the bathroom and start running the shower then help her strip off her clothes. My gaze rakes across her body as the memory of our night of passion wash over me: our lovemaking, the intensity between us, the way she ground herself against me. My mouth salivates at the sight of her full breasts bared before me. I lock eyes with her; I can see from the look in her eyes that she's aroused. The longing in my heart swells; I'm already certain that she's dripping wet down there. All I want is to fuck her now —to press my body against hers in the shower and lick her until she weakens onto the floor—but I need to be patient.

"Would you like me to help you, Elena? Do you need assistance showering?" She shakes her head quickly, biting her lip nervously. Her eyes plead with me to embrace her; I can see the desire burning within them. We both want each other desperately; I am desperate for her sweet pussy on my mouth now. But I restrain myself and step away from her. In an hour, I'll be making love to Elena as my wife. My darling, my everything. She climbs into the shower, shutting the door behind her. Resisting the urge to sit down on the toilet seat and watch her, I exit the bathroom, leaving the door ajar and glancing at the beautiful wedding gown she would soon be wearing. It has always been my dream: having Elena beside me in our bed and waking up next to her every day for the rest of my life. That's all I want--all that I yearned for--the only thing I truly desire: Elena by my side forever.

16

———————

Elena

After my shower, Elena helps me into the beautiful gown, then changes into the dress she's had made for herself. I can't help but stare--she looks radiant in a dress; she's always worn tight jeans and t-shirts with suspenders sometimes. Seeing Anna in this beautiful attire now all for me...I feel a plethora of emotions and desires for her when I should be trying to look for an escape route. Are her words true? If she doesn't leave with her father she'll be killed? And she won't leave without me? I'm struggling to make sense of the situation; it's simply too much and I don't know what to do. She grins when she notices my gaze as she spins around to show off her figure. Her flowing hair grazes past her shoulder and neckline, curled elegantly. I nervously run a brush through my hair, averting my eyes from her, trying not to stare. It is hard to believe; I am marrying Anna Stonewell yet, despite it not being my preferred option, I am not resistant to it.

Despite this chaos, I still love her. I ache for Anna just as much as before all the madness. What is wrong with me? Is it the aftereffects of being drugged? Or maybe it's Anna's mesmerizing spell. For some reason, she has a tight grip on me since I met her one year ago. Knowing that she had been watching me, scheming about our future together and wanting me, desiring me, loving me, deepens my craving for her. And this fierce monster between my legs, which I can't contain, makes things even harder. Why am I like this? Why do I have such a strong addiction to sex? My sexual appetite is out of control; it's as if I never get enough satisfaction. I need more of what I experienced from Anna last night. Anna interrupts my thoughts by seizing the brush from my hands and gliding her fingertips through my hair, softly kneading my scalp. I ought to push her away and tell her to get lost but instead, I arch my head back and lean into her.

"I'm going to give you a wonderful life, Elena. The steps you're taking to be with me are not taken lightly. You can still go to school, Elena. We'll start fresh together; I will help you study every day, whatever length of time it takes." She switches the massage from my head to my neck, tilting me back and leaning in close. Her lips touch mine in an electrifying kiss that steals my breath away and absorbs me in the aura of Anna's enchantment.

"But you'll be mine, Elena. Completely and utterly mine. I'm claiming you before we depart tomorrow night," she drawls as she brushes through my hair.

"Tomorrow night?" I query, watching her reflection in the vanity's mirror.

"My father's private jet leaves the ground at that time. We will be dead to the men he is severing ties with. I didn't choose this life, it chose me," she replies, her voice tinged with sorrow and regret.

"And we can never return here again?" Sliding off the

chair, I enquire hesitantly. My sweet Anna sets the brush down and places her hands firmly on my shoulders.

"No. We can confront them head-on but these gentlemen are highly influential. If I remain here, they will use me as a lure to get my father back but will inevitably kill me. This is a covenant written in blood; the only escape from it is death."

"By joining you, I have unknowingly committed myself to an inevitable demise," I remark bitterly; yet she does not argue, merely nodding in agreement.

"I told you, Elena; if you don't want to board that plane, I won't make you go," she murmurs, her eyes boring into mine. "But if I stay behind, they'll kill me within a week." Fire blazes in my gaze as I glower at her through the mirror.

"And do you really think I would let you die? Do you see the wedding gown draped on my body? Clearly, I'm not protesting." Snarling, I whirl around and face her.

Her lips curl up into a satisfied smile as she grabs my wrist and pulls me away from the vanity table. Accelerating towards the door handle she throws over her shoulder:

"Well then, you wouldn't mind marrying me right now."

"If you even think about fighting, Julian and Enzo will put you back to sleep--and I'll still marry you." My glare burns into her. Though I love her, she can be so maddeningly frustrating. Nodding reluctantly, I let her tug me away down the long stairway--we both are barefoot, our steps echoing off the beautiful marble foyer floor that became hardwood as we headed to the study.

The grandeur of the room, where Anna's father sits regally on an ornate throne-like chair, seems to sneer at me. His two henchmen flank our entryway; they share a striking resemblance with Anna. An excited thrill shoots through my veins as she confidently walks in, fingers holding onto my wrist. Then she glances back and nods to Enzo who steps forward and hands her a small black box.

"Elena," Anna beams, proudly introducing her siblings.

"These are my brothers, Angelo and Aberto - and of course, you already know my father." To the left of me, Angelo towers with a massive physique that contrasts the room's refined elegance. His dark brown hair is swept back into a ponytail, displaying a face as severe as it is handsome. He wears a tailor-made suit which highlights his imposing presence. Aberto, the other brother, is tall but leaner in muscularity with sinewy curves. His left arm boasts intricate tattoos and he sports cargo pants and a t-shirt that outlines every contour of his physique. His resemblance to Anna is more noticeable with the same dark wavy hair although his is cropped short and casually tied up in a bun with some loose strands framing his face and neck. Both greet me with smiles -Angelo's holding a hint of malevolence while Aberto's conveys an air of understanding, like he's aware of my distress.

"Anna," their father questions, his voice reverberating through the opulent room. "Are you certain about this? If you love her, you must know that claiming her brings a target to her back." His mirthful laugh fills the air. "The poor girl already had a mark the moment Anna began trailing her. My boss has informants keeping an eye on us all. If she leaves without her, they'll use her as bait to draw Anna back. Either way, they damn the lass." He snuffs out his cigar and stands upright, flanked by his sons as he strides for us. Anna steps in front of me, defensively shielding me with protectiveness that sends shivers down my spine.

"Aye, so territorial," her father remarks while standing in front of her. Yet Anna remains still. My fingers gripping at the material of her dress, my head spinning from deciphering the harrowing truth: Anna has been following me? My fate is sealed no matter what I do? Even if I run away there is already a curse on me. Whoever they're betraying by leaving will use me for bait to get Anna.

"They wouldn't harm her," Anna retorts, and her father shakes his head in disappointment. "They want a Stonewell, not her. They couldn't care less about our relationships."

"Anna, I raised you better. Trained you better. And I have warned you and your brothers that love makes you vulnerable. What are you prepared to do to save Elena?"

"Would you risk your life for hers?"

Anna holds her ground firmly as her authoritative father towers over her.

"I will lay down my life for Elena," she states resolutely; a testament to the unwavering faith of her conviction.

The conversation is abruptly halted when a woman strides into the room wearing a tailored black suit with a bible and folders tucked beneath her arm. I swivel to observe this newcomer while Anna moves protectively in front of me, creating an effective human wall between me and the rest of the room – evidently, Anna trusts no one in this room.

The woman garners attention with her curvaceous figure and cascading golden tresses. Her high-heeled shoes clicked against the floor in a beat that reverberates throughout the floor like an invisible pulse, radiating confidence wherever she moves. Her captivating blue eyes meet Anna's, prompting a smirk.

Anna lets out a groan. This woman is not welcomed here.

"Hello, Anna," The woman purrs. "It's a pleasure to see you."

Anna's father steps in front of her as if to shield her from the suggestive gaze. "Enough, Bianca. That's why we ended things. Making a pass at my daughter? You're predatory," he reprimands.

"She was eighteen when I made my move and quite obviously a lesbian. I was simply...curious," she retorts as she flicks her tongue across her lips for emphasis. He grunts indignantly, but she merely sighs and brushes him off, saying she has no time to banter with him.

"I don't have time to argue with you, I have a date, so let's get on with this," she declares.

Anna's father grins and gestures to his daughter. Bianca narrows her eyes in surprise—then he seizes her arm and commands, "You'll do me one last favor before we leave this place forever: marry my daughter."

Bianca tries to turn away, incredulous that he would force his own lesbian daughter to wed a man, but he held fast. "You're still going to try and force your lesbian daughter to marry a man? Not happening," she says firmly.

"Take another look, Bianca," he smirks. Anna tenderly tugs me from behind her, and Bianca's facial expression shifts from astonishment to a knowing grin.

"Well, she's quite the beauty, Anna. She's truly exquisite," she concedes, as Anna brings my hand up to her lips, kissing the back of it like it was hers. Bianca hands Enzo the folders and slides off her coat, examining the room.

"Let's get this show on the road then, shall we? And Anna," she takes a moment to appraise her with proud eyes, "It's gratifying to see that you didn't succumb to your father's wishes. You followed my advice. You took control of your life. I'm proud of you." Her words bring a lump in my throat. I sense an obscure parent-child relationship between them. I quickly shoot Anna a perplexed look, but she simply shrugs, pressing close to whisper into my ear.

"I'll explain later on. We needed someone for the ceremony and Bianca was our best choice at short notice. Marry
me, Elena." I give her an acrimonious glare; a brief thought
of slapping her across the face crosses my mind before
departing as quickly as it came. Instead of replying, I tear
my hand away and march with Bianca towards the corner of
the room where all will soon be said and done.

17

Anna

She marries me without hesitation, her gaze locking with mine as she says her vows without faltering. Tears roll down my cheeks and my hand trembles as I slide the wedding band on her finger. On the other hand, Elena is furious. After Bianca declares us wed, she steps towards me and plants a loving yet brief kiss on my lips.

"Congratulations." A soft voice drifts from Bianca's mouth, followed by a hug and gentle peck. She then whispers something in my ear, undoubtedly for Elena to hear.

"Call me if you ever want to play, Anna. I wouldn't mind if you brought your wife along either." A deep huff escapes Elena and her arms fold across her chest.

"May I go to bed now?" Elena growls before her unfolded hands move to cradle her wedding band. I scowl at Bianca who is clearly ruining my special night.

"Elena, I had a cake made for you and Anna. Will you stay and enjoy it with us?" My father asks, and as Bianca pulls away from my ear to grin wickedly at Elena, her jealousy was palpable. Rightly so – she thinks I love someone other than her. My father is correct about Bianca: she's always on the hunt for fresh meat. She had spotted me as a lesbian from miles away and tried to make a move, but he put an end to that. But in all reality, I owe her gratitude because she helped me come out as a lesbian and be true to myself; I've been strong-willed ever since. Yet if she thinks I'm going to give into temptation, then she's mistaken - I am devoted to Elena body and soul. All I really want right now is her naked beneath me as we make sweet love in our bedroom; however, for now I'll have a slice of cake with my father and take Elena upstairs afterwards. Oh, how I crave the taste of her lips. And perhaps a bit of rough-housing sex too; she struggles momentarily with me in anger that I allow Bianca to flirt so freely in front of her. So I wrap my arm around her waist, drawing her closer into me and say "Elena, don't be jealous - it's for nothing. I haven't been chasing after Bianca for months; it's been you who I've been pursuing relentlessly. Now let go of your rage and join us in having some cake – when we're finished, we can retreat to our bedroom and indulge in each other". Gasping softly, she places a hand over mine across her belly.

"This is too much, Anna. I'm exhausted and over-whelmed. You can't expect me to enjoy cake and party with your family like this was some planned extravagant wedding. I was forced into this." My glare meets her gaze.

"Were you, Elena? You could've said no." Her glare matches mine.

"Could I? And risk losing you forever? No. Plus you would have found a way to make me marry you," She snaps, then pushes my hand away with a hard slap. Shit, that hurt, but damn it was justified. She's pissed, hurt, and angry.

"Who are these people that will kill us if your father

leaves?" I shrug, because I don't know. I'm unaware of my father's business dealings. All I know is he has strong ties to the mafia and if he leaves, we're all dead to them.

"I'm a woman, Elena, raised in a male dominated world. What do you think they see me as? A woman whose place is to keep her mouth shut and look pretty for their usage. I'm not privy to my father's affairs, but what I do know is this world, which I never volunteered for, is dangerous. If my father says leaving means leaving it all behind, then I'll follow him. Because I've seen the extent of the horrors committed by those who work for him. My family made a deal with the devil a long time ago, and he's not finished collecting souls yet." Elena takes a deep breath and looks away from me towards the room before moving closer to me.

"I love you, Anna. I can't make these feelings go away, but you're not going to fuck me tonight. It'll be a long time before you even touch me like this again." She flashes me an evil smirk; as if she thinks she can punish me in such a way. If there's one thing I have control over, it's her pussy—always ravenous for an orgasm. She's talking mad shit because we won't make it through the night without that hungry monster between her legs and I'm just itching to bury my face between her legs and devour her sweet spot. My father gives Arnold a hand gesture and he nods before leaving the room. While I wait, I grip onto Elena's hand firmly despite her quiet resistance. There she goes again— telling me she loves me once more.

There's something inside my heart that can't be put into words right now. I just want to be alone with Elena, so I pull her closer, embracing her tightly. Eventually, she gives in, releasing a heavy sigh and resting against me. Aberto is busy talking with my father about something while Angelo casts

Elena an uninvited once-over; what an asshole! Everyone sees me as the dark one due to my vengeful kills and murderous ways, but even I don't match up to him - he's a real monster. He gets pleasure from torturing his victims whereas I see it as putting them out of their misery. I kill for revenge whereas he does it for the enjoyment. I don't like the way Angelo's looking at my wife - out of everyone in my family if there was one person I'd love to take out, it'd be him. After all, how many messes has my father had to clean up because of him? My father knows about my kills but doesn't speak on it - he's aware that I know how to get rid of the problem efficiently. It's almost a pity for whoever this guy has chosen to spend his life with. He adjusts his belt buckle then walks towards Elena while I glare at him, prepared to take action.

We have an acrimonious relationship, our arguments about my sexuality are much worse than those with my father. Angelo wanted to marry me off to his friend and he was willing to try anything to make it happen - threatening and even trying to hurt me - until he discovered the real reason my father sent me away every summer since I was six. He wanted me to learn how to defend myself from the monstrous men in our society. Now I can protect Elena from them. Starting with my own family, those veritable bloodsuckers.

"You are now a Stonewell, Elena," Angelo says before licking his lips at her hungrily. She glances toward me fearfully; she has seen what I can do when I took Jack down quickly, ready to shoot him right in front of his friends. How would she respond if I blew my brother's brains out in front of her? My anticipation rises as I lick my own lips. Angelo notices my lethal expression and grins wickedly.

"Oh, lighten up, Anna. I'm just getting to know my new

sister-in-law; after all, you brought her into this family—it's best she gets to know us better." I am ready to rip his fucking head off his shoulders! This is the game he wants to play? So be it. But Elena is not community property.

Suddenly, Arnold enters the room with a cart holding a three-tier, all-black wedding cake—my father knows black is my favorite color, but blue for my sweet wife would have been preferable. Elena's eyes follow the cake as Arnold pushes it in front of us with a large knife resting beside it. I clench my hands tightly, fighting the urge to stab him in the neck with it. My father approaches the cake, standing before us and grabbing a plate.

"Elena, while this isn't the wedding I'd wished for my daughter, I'm still happy to see her married nonetheless. Congratulations, daughter-in-law and welcome to the family." Elena feigns a smile as my father holds out one of the small cake plates for her.

"Will you do the honor of cutting your wedding cake?" Elena's eyes are unreadable as she stares down at the knife. Angelo is much more protective of our father than us; he demands absolute respect, and anything less is unacceptable. Though he can't seem to control me; it always ends with him on the floor and my foot on his neck. He may be twice my size, but I can take him down effortlessly. Angelo's smile quickly fades into a glare as he steps right into Elena's face, ready to intimidate her.

"My father asked you to cut your cake – don't dishonor him," he growls. Elena gazes up at him fearlessly. Wow, my sweetheart never fails to astonish me.

"Get away from me!" Elena hisses at him. His ego has been crushed, bested by a woman yet again. He lifts his hand, ready to strike her, but I seize it before it can fly towards her face, too quick for Elena to understand what is happening. I grasp the knife and shove it into his hand, piercing the steel rolling crate that the cake sits on. Angelo shrieks and whimpers like a pup while Elena watches, her expression slightly delighted with my handy work. She looks up at me with admiration, not dread this time. Would she give me a gift of open arms and let me savor her sweetest spot? I salivate, awaiting my reward. Arnold leaves the room suddenly, almost as if he's aware he must tidy up soon, but surprisingly he's only gone a short time, coming back with a new blade and presenting it to me while Angelo keeps shrieking in pain, desperately attempting to yank the knife from his hand. Blood trickles onto the carpeting and into the cake, however my father doesn't appear perturbed by it all. Actually, he seems happy about it. He holds out his dish to Elena once again.

"May I have my piece now?" he asks her cheerfully, flashing a wide grin. Elena shrugs and glances at me and I give her the knife.

"You're insane. You're all insane," Elena mutters as she takes the knife and cuts into the wedding cake. Aberto and Bianca clap in response, and soon they are lined up to get their own slice of the delicious dessert. I will release my brother from his torment shortly, but for now I am content to let him suffer a little longer. In reply to her comment, we all just shrug our shoulders; this is what it means to be a Stonewell—we take pride in who we are and don't apologize for it. Looking into her beautiful olive eyes, I simply give Elena a knowing shrug and smile—taking a slice of cake she's cut and served on one of the cake plates, I take a bite, enjoying the flavor of my wedding cake.

18

———

Elena

The more time passes, the crazier it gets. Anna is out of control; she doesn't need to be in jail; she needs to be hidden from society for life. How many people will she kill during her lifetime? She seems unopposed to killing. I can't help but believe her. Anna pulls me away into the bedroom carrying a plate with a large slice of the wedding cake. She looks at me with an unnerving smile while eating the cake as if it was her last meal. She doesn't try to hide her happiness with being my wife despite all the crying and begging from other women who would murder to be in my place and yet here I am, desperate for knowledge about what this means for my future, trapped in a marriage with Anna Stonewell - the woman who's been watching me for months without approaching me until now. Why did she have to wait? Anna holds out a fork full of cake for me.

"Here, honey. Try it. It tastes delicious." I reluctantly

open my mouth and let her feed me the cake. It's delicious, and I close my eyes, savoring the taste of it. But it's not enough. I need to know where this is going. She's so happy, even though she just stabbed her brother right through the hand for me. What won't this woman do? She takes her finger and rubs away some of the chocolate lingering from my lips, taking it in with her finger.

"Anna, what now?" She gives me a mischievous look, and my core throbs with anticipation for her to taste me, to take me - yet I have to keep a clear head.

"No, Anna. We can't do that." She narrows her eyes at me, setting the plate down at the end table before quickly wrapping her arms around my waist, pulling me into her embrace.

"We can't what? Elena? Make love? You're my wife now, why can't I make love to my wife?" I glare at her incredulously - is she serious right now?

"I'm a prisoner." She shakes her head, biting her lips as she gently rubs her hands up and down my back.

"You're not a prisoner, Elena. You're my wife. There's a difference.

You've been planning a future with me all this time? Yet, you saw the way I looked at you - if you've been watching me as much as you say - you know how I felt about you." Anna shrugs and backs away, seemingly irritated with me.

"FINE!" She snaps, going over to the closet before retrieving a nightgown and tossing it at me. I catch it, clutching it to my stomach before it falls.

"You should change for bed. We have one more stop before our flight leaves tomorrow night." I throw the night gown to the floor, and storm over to her as she pulls clothes from her closet shelves. I grasp her arm, making her face me. Her eyes widen in shock when she sees my rage.

"I gave up my entire FUCKING life for you! Don't you ever snap at me like that again!" I shout furiously at her.

"Alright, Elena, calm down." She yanks her arm away from me and removes her dress, letting it drop to the ground, leaving her in just her bra and panties.

"You rejected me. How am I supposed to feel on our wedding night?" Oh, my god, she is insane.

"At least tell me where I'm going; I'm leaving my life here." Anna slips on her tank top before facing me.

"What life, Elena? You go to school, work hard, eat little and sleep less. That's living?" Her words cut into me so I step back and grab the night gown. She sighs then moves towards me but I move away from her, retreating to the other side of the bed.

"I want to go to sleep. Maybe I just need time or something." I turn away from her and undress, sliding on the night gown, then quickly climb into bed, turning my back to her. I hear her groaning, but she switches off the lights and climbs into bed with me, snuggling close, her hands gliding along the fabric of my night gown that fitted closely against my ass.

"Elena. There are things I know about you that you likely don't understand yourself. I want to shove her hands aside from my ass but I can't. My pussy is begging for her right now. What the hell? What is wrong with me? Why do I always need to have an orgasm all the damn time?

"You need me, Elena. You won't be able to sleep until you climax. I know you can't rest without a good orgasm." My eyes open wide and I stare at her in shock.

"How do you know that?" Anna smiles wickedly, quickly shifting herself so she's straddling me, spreading my legs.

"I watched you every night, Elena. I had cameras installed in your apartment while you were away at school.

If I couldn't be there with you physically, I'd watch you. It wasn't until I started watching the footage that I noticed you masturbating almost every night, just to get to sleep. But now you have me, Elena. You'll come in my mouth—and it will happen regularly."

I gasp at her words, trying to resist her, but my hands are gripping the sheets, bracing myself for something my body needs. She pulls my breasts from the cups of my nightgown and devours them with her mouth, pushing them together as she takes both into her mouth. My back arches uncontrollably as I give in to her because all I want is to feel. Anna isn't wrong; I crave her touch. My head thrashes from side to side, trying not to orgasm from the way she teases my breasts alone. The way she squeezes my nipples and flicks her tongue over them is like being ensnared by passion—I need it; I need her.

"You're like a drug, Elena," she whispers against my lips. "I'll never have enough—never get enough of you." My legs part as she pushes her body against me and I lose myself in the sensation. All I can do is feel—feel her curves against mine, feel every movement of her mouth against my skin. She moves from my neck to my breasts, then back to my lips, sealing us with a passionate kiss that has my head spinning. Our tongues tangle, and I grasp her face, burying my hands into her hair, trying to ingest all of her into me. She's fucking mine! This feral possessive hunger I have for Anna is ravaging me. The taste of her is divine, her lips sweet like candy but still imbued with the flavor of our chocolate wedding cake. In this moment, it doesn't matter why she chose me; I'm just grateful she did—grateful she's keeping me.

"I love you, Elena. I'm so happy you're now mine—all of you." Her lips whisper against mine and I moan, gripping her hips as she rocks into me. Desiring to feel her skin pressing against mine, I tug on her tank top and she chuckles, lifting it off then quickly discarding her bra. Her mouth meets mine, her nipples grazing my chest, and I can sense her tugging at her panties, sliding them down before kicking them away and sending the fabric to the floor. My palms travel to her breasts, cupping them while brushing my thumb across her nipples; she gasps, moans, and smiles between our lips, deepening the kiss between us as she grinds into me. Her hands move between my legs with force, ripping apart my panties before slipping them off me and flinging them to the floor; then she fondles my pussy gently with her fingers running up and down my slit, feeling the glistening wetness caused by my pleasure coating me.

"You're drenched, Elena. Why would I let you go to sleep like this?" I groan against her lips, luring her into a deeper kiss as she slides two fingers deep inside me, thrusting them in and out of me. That's the problem, Anna. I always crave satisfaction. I'm never fulfilled. I'm always craving more sensation. It's never enough, I constantly want more--constantly yearning for it. During the last year, I've dreamed of moments such as this with Anna--the way she's ravishing me, kissing me, expressing her adoration; it's all coming into fruition like a dream. I press myself against her, synchronizing our movement, letting her take what she wishes from me. She curves her digits inside of me, sliding them from side to side, hitting every single sweet spot. Oh my gosh! My mouth gapes open, my breath halts, my eyes move backwards into my skull as my orgasm slams into me like a tidal wave and my body jolts underneath her. She has smile of sheer delight in her gaze; simply delighted to watch me reach my climax beneath her.

"That's right, Elena. come on me, baby. I need to feel you

explode all over my fingers. My walls contract, my orgasm obliterates me as she continues to thrust in and out of me, draining the orgasm out of me. When she's satisfied, she drags her fingers out of me and inserts them in her mouth, forcing me to watch as she licks them clean, savoring the taste of my orgasm. Her eyes hungrily scan over me as I take some time to catch my breath; my entire body still hot from the intense climax she just gave me.

"I haven't had enough of you yet, Elena. You taste divine. May I have more?" My eyes widen as I watch her place herself between my legs, opening them wide and not breaking eye contact for a moment. I raise my head to observe her as she trails her tongue along my wet folds. She firmly grasps my thighs as I buck against her, struggling to escape the waves of pleasure rolling over me. Then she unceremoniously inserts her tongue inside me, thrusting in and out; my hand slides down to grab the back of her head, pushing her harder into me, wanting even more. Her head moves rhythmically from side to side while her tongue pierces deeply into me, hitting all the precise spots and sending me hurtling into ecstasy. How does she know exactly how to pleasure me so well? I scream, grinding hard against her mouth just before another orgasm explodes within me, radiating heat throughout my body. Anna refuses to let go, keeping up with each of my spasms. Exhausted, I smash my hands down on the bed and scream out once again in sheer bliss. Anna slowly lifts up and kisses my thigh tenderly, running her tongue along it before nibbling it softly.

"That should help you sleep peacefully now," she murmurs with a smug smirk on her face before curling up beside me under the covers. I give her a stern gaze and she squints at me inquisitively, wondering what's on my mind: that she won't be going to sleep without me fucking her tonight!

19

Anna

Elena is mine in every way, and this moment, making love to her just confirmed that. She'll never be rid of me. NEVER. But she scowls at me, clearly displeased about something. Had I not pleasured her properly? Should I bury my head between her legs again? My bigger plans for us in the bedroom once we get to our new home are already set, however right now, my goal was simply to make sure she has a restful night's sleep. There's one thing I want us to achieve before leaving Michigan for good. Elena needs to say her last goodbye to her mother. I'm not disclosing our destination until we're near Brookside, which is when I know she'll begin to understand what I have planned. Elena's relationship with her mother is rocky. The last time I saw them together was during Thanksgiving break when I followed her to Brookside. They had a intense argument over dinner - something I wish I hadn't heard - but it wrecked Elena. She left her mother and hasn't been back since. Elena's mother hates the fact that she's gay and it goes against everything her mother taught her as she is fiercely religious; she won't waver from it, not even for her daughter. As far as Elena's mother is concerned, so long as she remains queer, she's dead to her.

"Elena?" I call out aloud, wondering why she was so irritated with me.

"Oh no, you're not getting away that easily. It's my turn now!" she cries out, throwing the sheets off her body. I let out a gasp and my eyes widen in surprise as I smile at her. After all she's been through today, I thought sex would just be to help her relax and fall asleep, but here she is wanting to pleasure me.

"Elena wait!" I try to say, but it's too late; she straddles me and begins to strip off her dress, leaving herself fully exposed before me. My mouth waters as I admire her beautiful breasts, wishing for nothing more than to latch onto them once again. She pulls her hair back into a bun, securing it and then dives down to press her lips against mine. I gasp in delight as our tongues dance together with passion. When she grinds against me, I can feel her wet pussy brush up against my clit and it feels incredible. There's no way for me to win this battle – Elena has made it known that she wants to fuck me, so fuck me she will!

"I wanna make you scream," she whispers between kisses. "I wanna see you shake." My eyes widen even further with awe as I look at her – how is it possible for me not to be obsessed with this woman? The more she touches me, shows me love and kisses me...the deeper down the rabbit hole of obsession I go. An understatement when saying I'm obsessed with Elena – if it were at all possible, I'd take her soul with me so that we could be together forever in the afterlife. No other woman on this planet will ever compare to her.

"Ah, fuck, Elena." I moan as her teeth sink into my ear. She kneads and massages my breasts, teasing my nipples with her fingertips, sending me spiraling into excitement. When she pulls away from my neck, she roughly nips my lip, leaving an imprint of herself behind. Her lips travel down my body, luxuriating in the skin beneath her tongue before settling between my chest. She gazes up at me with eyes filled to the brim with desire. I savor the taste of her on my mouth, then arch my head back in pleasure when her hands encase my breasts, taking them one by one into her mouth. Is this what she had imagined? Everything about this intimate moment suggests it has been a long time coming; however, in turn, she's unleashing something much more powerful than she expected. With every passing second, I'm becoming increasingly desperate for her touch. Moving away from my chest, she rubs her breasts against mine while grinding against me and that's when I can no longer control the fires raging within me. I clench her waist, attempting to position her exactly where I need her to be, but she refuses, snatching my hands and forcing them above my head to restrain me. If I didn't like it so much, I could easily overpower her; however, right now I'm content in allowing her to have power over me.

"No!" She snarls at me, but I smile and raise my head to kiss her. She steps away from me, her gaze shifting hungrily between my legs. Keeping a firm grip on my thighs, she bends down and starts devouring my pussy with intention, as though she's been planning this all along. Desperate to keep myself in check, I grasp the sheets tightly and bite down on my lip until I feel it might break the skin. Elena licks and bites at my swollen clit and suddenly curses start pouring out of me uncontrollably. No matter how hard I try, I can't fight against the urge to grab her and pull her off me.

Her tongue finds its way deep inside me, pushing against my walls while her face is pressed firmly against my pussy.

"Elena!" I beg her, and it's then that she slides her tongue from my clit down to my entrance before shoving it inside me and pressing her face against me. My body quakes as I feel like I'm about to explode.

"Fuck!" I scream, coming instantly under her touch. This is the most powerful orgasm I've ever experienced. She's taken hold of me and completely drained me; whatever will I had to restrain myself with this woman dissipates in an instant. She continues pleasuring me with her tongue, savoring the juices from my climax. She looks up with a proud grin smeared across her face, mouth glistening with my come. Then she lifts my leg over her shoulder, trapping her body between mine so that our pussies are joined together. She moves against me, brushing her clit against mine - it's like all my fantasies are coming true with her. My back arches and my hips drive into the bed as I match her thrusts. It's so damn perfect and erotic at once.

"Elena, oh my God, please!" She closes her eyes and shakes her head no, tilting her head back - she's close, so incredibly close - skin on skin, our clits rubbing each other as they send me rocketing over the edge again. I cry out as my orgasm explodes through me, and Elena follows suit, moaning and screaming as her entire body shudders from the intensity of our moment together. I want more of her. When we're done, she collapses on top of me, our sweaty bodies entwined together. I hug her tightly.

"I'm going with you, Anna. As much as I want to, I can't fight this. I can't deny loving you, wanting you, needing you." I tenderly run a hand over her perspiring forehead, lightly pressing soft kisses on it, so she knows that I understand. She's coming with me in any case, voluntarily or kicking and screaming, yet to realize that she picks me now implies everything to me.

"How will I know you won't tire of me like you did with Alexa and Samantha? They are begging for your love, yet you abandon them for me." I groan, not expecting to even consider those ladies at present. After the second we just shared, it's annoying me that she would think I'd cast her away when she's all that really matters. I need to shake her silly, or better yet, discipline her pussy with a firm fuck for even having that idea. What will it take for Elena to understand she owns me in every way possible? I inhale profoundly and attempt to quiet myself down. The last thing I need is to alarm her, however that may be my smartest option right now. Since Elena is mine. I'm not contending with her about that.

"Elena, I appreciate Alexa and Samantha's companionship. It's you that I love. I've loved you since the first moment I saw you. I've watched over you for some time, kept you safe." She attempts to move her body off of me; however, I don't let her.

"Elena, I can't bear the thought of not being with you. When it was time for my family to leave, taking you along was inevitable; whether you loved me or not, I'll still be there for you. I love you Elena and that's all that matters. But if staying here is what you want, just let me know and I'll fight for us. You name it and I'll do whatever it takes - leaving isn't an option." She shifted above me in a straddle and placed a hand over my heart.

"Going means leaving school, Anna. That's all I have here; no family and only one friend besides Mrs. Laura at the apartment."

"You have me now, Elena," tears start to pour out from her eyes.

"I don't want to lose you either, Anna. So, I'll come with you." Her lips curves into a mischievous smile as she narrows her eyes at me "Kicking or screaming? Really?" I shrug, feeling the warmth of multiple orgasms racing through my body.

"It's time to go to bed, Elena. We've got a long day ahead of us tomorrow." She nods, getting down from me, but I keep her close, snuggling against her. She trusts me, my sweet Elena. She may not understand yet that I will do anything for her, but she'll learn in time. We have forever to spend together, and I won't deprive her of wanting an education. We can start anew; if she wishes, she can return to school. We'll study alongside each other, and I will learn whatever it is that she wants to study. Elena was taking up journalism with a minor in history. I'm thankful for failing that economics class – although I would have found another way to get close to her. Being near was like air for me; now that she's mine, I'm never going to let her go. Just one last arrangement and we can leave this place behind to start a life in paradise; there's nothing I won't give Elena – apart from parting from her. Soon enough she peacefully drifts off in my arms, her warm body naked against mine and the aroma of our love lingering on us and in the air. This is what I'd like to do for the rest of my days – keep her naked body by my side – without it I won't be able to sleep anymore. She's all of me, forever, and nothing will ever take her away from me... not even death.

20

Elena

Anna won't tell me where we are going, but she's got me in this expensive SUV -- different from the one she usually drives. Damn, just how rich are they? Anna climbs in, wearing her signature getup: a fitted t-shirt with tight ripped jeans that hug her curvy waist. Her hair is down -- I know only because she knows how much I love it when she does. She looks at me and grins seductively as she starts the engine. Then she leans in and steals a kiss from me; I don't deny her. The smell of her is heavenly. She pulls closer, deepening the kiss between us. I find myself lost in the moment, just enjoying her lips on mine before she breaks away and stares back at me.

"Elena," she tells me, "I want you to know how much I love you." But that love plea doesn't sound all too convincing. What's she up to? Where is she taking me? She notices my glare and smiles as she starts the engine and pulls out of the garage.

"Where are you taking me?" I demand as she drives me out of Bayshore and into the city. I can't help but notice a gaggle of police officers surrounding the diner where I used to work, my gaze transfixed to the window as we pass by. Anna appears to speed up as if trying to avoid being caught at the light. She doesn't even glance in that direction — how could she not be curious? I study her nervously, wondering if she had anything to do with why the police are there. Sure, my boss Jordan was a major jerk, but he wasn't murder worthy. Are they already plotting to kill her for leaving town? A million thoughts race through my mind and I shudder.

"Can we stop by the diner?" I ask her, urgency tinging my voice. "I want to know what happened." She keeps driving ahead, refusing to engage me with her eyes.

"Anna, I asked you..."

"No. We can't stop by the diner, Elena. There's nothing to see." The pieces fall into place — yes, Anna knows the reason behind why the police are there. I draw in a deep breath, watching as the diner eventually fades from view.

"What happened?" I insist again. She groans and finally meets my hard stare with her own.

"You don't want to know, Elena." I glare at her stubbornly and retort: "I want you to tell me — right now!" Taking her eyes off me for a brief moment, she finally relents: "Alright, Elena. Since you're insistent, I'll tell you. I took care of a personal matter there...with your boss Jordan." Personal matter? How does she know?

"What did you do to him?" She stops at a light and turns, glaring at me.

"I took care of him. He was watching you change through a peephole in the diner's restroom. I put a stop to that months ago, but I thought to myself, what kind of monster would I be if I left him to attack another unsuspecting woman?" I gasp, looking away from her.

"Did you kill him?" I ask her. She doesn't answer me.

"It's better you know nothing, Elena." I sit back in my seat, trying to stifle the tears that fall from my face. I have blood on my hands. I was right about Anna; she isn't opposed to killing anyone.

"Elena, you are my entire world. When I tell you I've been watching you since the day I first saw you at the university, I meant it; I meant every word, sweetheart. Jordan was watching you, and when he started following you, I stepped in. I made sure he never bothered you again."

"But did you have to kill him though?" She glares at me.

"Why are you weeping for him? Did you feel something for him?" I glare back at her, wiping the tears from my face. This isn't about Jordan; this is about her. And I can't believe she's jealous. *Is she serious right now?*

"You're an asshole!" She laughs, turning her eyes back to the road.

"All the better he's dead then," she says.

"Sharing you. is not an option Elena. I'll kill anyone who gets in the way of loving you."

"So, you did kill him!" She doesn't answer me; she keeps driving, and it isn't until we reach Brookside that it dawns on me where we are heading.

"No Anna," I say pleadingly. "Please turn around." But she ignores me, driving right past the city's welcome sign.

"Are you going to hurt my mother?" I ask her nervously. She glares at me, then grins wickedly.

"Only if she makes me, Elena." I tug at the passenger door, but it's locked from the inside.

"Let me out! Now!" I shout at her. She ignores me,

continuing on our path to my mother's place. What is she up to? Why do I have to see my mother?

"I know about your relationship with your mom, Elena. I followed you when you visited her last Thanksgiving. I observed from afar and witnessed your argument with one another. How you pleaded for your mother to love you, yet she could not look beyond her convictions. I saw how it pained you, and I watched as you ran off in the middle of the night. I followed you, making sure that you arrived home safely, then witnessed your tears as you drifted asleep." Speechless, the rest of the drive passes without a word between us. She had been tracking me all this time? I nervously run a hand through my hair because honestly, I don't know what to say.

"Please don't hurt my mother." She groans, pulling the car over onto the shoulder of the road.

"I don't want to hurt your mother, Elena. I only want you to say goodbye." I stare at her, tears streaming down my face, unable to fight them back any longer. In truth, I don't want to see her. She told me I was dead to her.

"Can't I just say it over the phone?" Anna reaches out and tenderly strokes my cheeks, wiping away the tears.

"Elena, do it for me. Say goodbye to your mother. If my mother were still alive, I'd never want to leave without seeing her one last time." Her words nearly take my breath away. Tales of her mother passing from cancer when she was very young had been whispered in hushed tones around town, but I hadn't dared bring it up; not wanting to injure an old wound again.

"But if she does something wrong, you won't hesitate to hurt my mother?" I question her while she rolls her eyes and put the car into drive once more.

"Elena sweetheart, I'm madly in love with you: heavy

emphasis on MAD! You're beautiful, and you mean the world to me. Not even my father would be off limits if it came down to it." My gasp fills the car as Anna drives us to my mother's house--the reality that this could be our last goodbye finally sinking in hard. How can I tell her no now? It's becoming clear that she's right: if I'm going off the radar, there can't be room left for second-thoughts about my mother...I need to let go and leave everything behind; no second thoughts allowed.

"You may despise me now, Elena, but I can assure you that you'll soon love me. I'm doing this all for your sake." In response to her words, my heart swells. She's doing this all for me; every single thing, only for me.

"Oh, Anna," I breathe out, clasping her hand. She grabs hold of my wrist and draws my arm to her lips, planting a kiss on the back of it.

"I can't believe that you followed me here. It's creepy beyond measure, yet somehow I find it flattering." She kisses the back of my hand once more.

"The stalking doesn't finish here, Elena." Anna replies with the faintest of smiles curling upon her lips. "I will probably keep on following you forever, because you have become my object of longing." I narrow my eyes at her in confusion. How am I any different from Alexa or Samantha? But she had gotten so mad when I had asked about them before--so I decide against bringing it up again.

"You'll tire from loving me," I deadpan with a sigh. Anna bursts out in laughter as we turn onto my mother's street -- my anxiety levels rising steadily as we get closer to seeing my mother after my heated argument with her this past Thanksgiving.

"That's what you don't understand," she starts slowly,

coming to a stop at the trailer park with her over-the-top vehicle--it stands out amongst the rest like a sore thumb.

"My obsession for you runs deep and wide; far beyond what meets the eye. I'll never tire for you, sweetheart. More than likely, it will be you that tires of me."

"That's impossible," I tell her right away while shaking my head. "I'm just as smitten with you as much as ever." Pulling into the trailer park driveway, Anna looks around before turning towards me again with a serious expression on her face.

"Anna, please don't do this..." My voice trails off but she completely ignores me and continues talking regardless.

"Today, you will introduce me to your mother as your wife." With an exasperated groan escaping through my lips, I helplessly agree to comply.

"She hates the fact that I'm a lesbian. Introducing you to her will just anger her more," I say, while Anna parks her car in front of my mother's trailer. Neighbors peep through their windows and open their doors, wondering why such an expensive vehicle was in front of my mother's home.

I yank on the door after she stops the engine—glaring at her because she refuses to unlock it.

"Elena, I'd like to talk about this with you. Now that we're married, there won't be any problems with me pampering you." My glare intensifies.

"It isn't the 1950s anymore, Anna. Chivalry is dead." She glares back at me.

"I don't care what year it is—you're my wife! Can't I have this?" I inhale deeply and nod reluctantly, wanting to get out of this trailer park as soon as possible. A victorious smile graces her face—as if she had just won a battle. I roll my eyes as she steps out of the car and walks around to the passenger side to open my door, offering her hand for me to take when I unbuckle my seatbelt.

"This isn't going to go well, Anna; and I never had a great relationship with my mom to begin with. My childhood wasn't easy." I bet she doesn't know that part—but then again, crazy as she is, perhaps she does.

"I want you to say goodbye, Elena. Cause I'm never giving you back." A thrill of anticipation runs through me as she says this; the warmth between my legs tells me why. She watches me shift, aware of the ache she put there. Her words have a way of taking my breath away - and not just with their romanticism. Then she pulls me closer and kisses me right in front of the whole neighborhood. As if they don't already know! Growing up here, all of Brookside knew I was gay. Some kind of osmosis, probably. My mother probably told them at the rundown community center out of frustration. Most people around here get stuck in poverty; born into it, they die in it. But not me - I decided early on that I'd find a way out of this place. Ironically enough, that's how I stumbled across Anna: beautiful and dangerous, and being swept off my feet by her with her beauty and charming ways. I squeeze her hand tight as she breaks our kiss and walks me to my mother's door.

21

Anna

I'm surprised her mother bothered to open the door for Elena, and she steps in eagerly. I follow behind her, giving Elena's mother a polite nod as I pass. She gives me a glare of contempt, taking note of my presence. I stand beside Elena, staring in awe—Elena looks just like her mother, though the cigarette in her hand might explain why she appears more haggard than usual. Her mother's hair is long and beautiful yet thinning with gray streaks around the edges. Her face and neck are wrinkled, with age spots dotted along them. Unfortunately, despite being clean, the trailer reeks of cigarette smoke and alcohol. Elena focuses on her mother uneasily and swallows hard; she's surprisingly small - the same height as Elena, but far friendlier in frame due to her poor dieting habits. It wouldn't be a problem anymore though; I'll make sure of that - no more sitting idle while she wastes away. Similarly, I've taken care of Mrs. Laura too; from now on, she'd live out her days in comfort and tranquility.

"Mom," Elena begins hesitantly, before her mother cuts across.

"What do you want? Did you come here to apologize?" At this point, Elena's mother notices me properly for the first time and scowls at us both before putting out her cigarette. "Who's your rich friend?"

Elena holds up our entwined hands and I allowed myself to give a soft smile.

"Ms. Allen," I say politely. "It's a pleasure meeting you. My name is Anna Stonewell."

Elena blushes before speaking again: "She's my wife, mother." Though her mother still glares at us both suspiciously, she makes no further comment on it. "A Stonewell, huh? That means you're rich?" I force a smile at her question despite the feel of anger boiling in me.

"Don't call me mom. You don't have that right anymore," my heart sinks as I watch the hurt in Elena's face. Bringing her here was to ensure she'd have no regrets, but it looks like I'm the one with all the regrets now. Maybe I shouldn't have come at all. Elena drops her head, trying to hide her tears of disappointment from me.

"Elena, it's time for you to go. Don't you want to say goodbye to your daughter?" Sonya Allen, Elena's mother, smiles maliciously at me. It makes me want to slam the smirk off her face - or better yet put a bullet through her skull. She wasn't exactly mother-of-the-year material when it came to Elena; she resented her resilience and hated her because she reminded her of her father.

"This gay bitch isn't my daughter, "Sonya says sharply, and Elena's head whips up, glaring furiously at her mother as if ready to shield me from any harm.

"Don't talk to my wife like that!"

Elena tenses up as soon as her mom raises her hand,

preparing for an intense slap that never comes as I catch Sonya by the wrist, twisting her arm behind her back. Elena's eyes widen in shock, gasping out "Anna, no!"

The rage inside me reaches a boiling point and I wrench Sonya's arm harder, relishing the screams of pain that escape her lips as I push her face against the wall.

"You'll never hit her again." I hiss viciously into Sonya's ear before releasing my grip on the arm twisted behind her back.

"And you're right Elena is dead to you - that's why I brought her here."

"Anna, please! Let her go. Please! I'm begging you!" Elena pleads with me, but I can't listen right now. I want to reach for my gun, but I've left it in my car on purpose. There is no way I can watch someone hurting my wife.

"Elena, say goodbye to your mother," I say firmly. She quickly stifles her sobs, knowing that I'm bluffing.

"Goodbye, mom," Elena whispers before walking towards the door and opening it.

"Anna, get me out of here," she begs me as I release her mother. Her mother holds her arm and winces, leaning against the wall.

"You're dead to me Elena! Don't come back here ever again!" she screams at us over and over as we start walking towards the car. Elena yanks away from me once we reach the passenger door; she doesn't wait for me to open it, instead climbing in straightaway. I choose not to quarrel with her and step aside, watching as she pulls the door closed. Her mother's voice shrieks hateful words loud enough for the whole neighborhood to hear, but Elena keeps her gaze forward with arms crossed over her chest as I enter the car. We have two hours until our plane departs; our bags are already being loaded on board.

"Get me out of here." She gasps, struggling to catch her breath. I give her a sorrowful look, knowing that I should have heeded her when she had spoken before about her mother's hurtful words. I feel regretful for making her relive them again, but I wanted her to be free of any guilt. Starting the engine, I pull away quickly from the trailer park, driving away from the city until we make our exit. Immediately, Elena releases a long exhale and clutches at her chest as if she's having a panic attack.

"Elena!" I cry out in fear.

"Pull over! Please, just pull over for one second!" She screams shrilly. Quickly, I stop the car and help her out; she races a few feet away then collapses on her knees wailing uncontrollably. Following behind, I kneel beside her and embrace her tightly as she finally lets go of all sadness in despair. I hold her closely, whispering comforting words in her ear while rocking gently until she calms down from sobbing. When she turns around to nestle in my arms again with the encouragement of my love, I notice her reddened eyes and swollen face still drenched with tears.

"I love you, Elena. I'm so sorry," I say softly as I hug her closer to me.

"I love you, too, Anna." She chokes out, "This is it. I don't have anyone else; just you. If you leave me, it will kill me. I don't even have a reason to stay alive without you." Her words evoke fear and fury in me and my arms tighten around her.

"Elena, I'll never leave you. I'll never let you go, baby." She looks up at me as if she's struggling to trust my words. That's okay. I'll spend the rest of my life showing her how much she means to me.

"Take me away from here. I don't ever want to see this place again; you're offering me a fresh start--free of the past-

-with you." She reaches forward with a shaky hand and gently brushes my cheek. A tear escapes me; I can't help it. My wife is in so much pain and it kills me to watch it. I lift her up carefully and help her into the car before rushing around to the driver's side and quickly speed off towards the airport.

"Do you want to stop by Laura..."

"No," she says quickly cutting me off. "I won't ask how you know Mrs. Laura, and honestly, I don't even want to know. Just make sure she's taken care of; she was my friend." I smile nervously at her as we speed through the city towards our destination.

"It's already handled; Laura has been moved to a luxury senior village where she can spend the remainder of her days comfortably." Elena keeps her eyes turned away from mine, focused ahead on the long road in front of us.

"Good. I'm ready, Anna," Elena commands. We drive faster, and my urge is to grab her hand and tell her how much I love her, but I'll do it on the jet. When we arrive at the airport, I pull onto the private road toward the jet that's open and waiting for us. We're early, so there's no time for hesitation. If Elena even pauses, she'll sleep during the whole ride. She agreed to go on a date with me and this decision was solidified; I'm not leaving without her. Though it would be possible if she denied me, we are too far gone now. Pulling up to the plane, I turn off the engine and step out, handing the pilot my keys. We won't see that car again. Elena doesn't look back as she wastes no time boarding the plane. Smiling, I follow her to watch her make something to eat from the buffet while admiring our private jet's beauty: complete with a bedroom, bathroom and shower! This is my father's plane - one he'll probably discard once we land at our destination of starting our new life without any connections to crime. All our money is clean and soon, our identities will be wiped clean too - though even my brothers don't know this location.

She hastily fixes herself a sandwich, hungry after an evening of lovemaking and the pressure of handling her mother. I only wish to embrace her, yet I desire to give her time to adjust.

"Elena," She gazes at me, wiping her face.

"I don't want to speak about it." She retorts sharply, and I let it go. Her eyes scan around the jet once more, evidently captivated.

"This is my future now. A life of extravagance?" I smirk at her and I can't help myself. The need to caress her tear-streaked face is too strong. I stroke her cheek tenderly.

"The only thing I won't permit you, Elena is leaving me." She rolls her eyes at me and takes a bite out of her sub.

"Who said something about desiring to leave you, Anna? Isn't it clear? I'm as mad as you are. I can't exist without you either." Elena kicks off her heels, obviously irritated by their feel. I know how much she detests wearing high heels and how uncomfortable they are on her feet, but I made her wear them because I wanted to massage her feet afterwards. Damn, even as my wife, I'm still doing wild stuff, my need to have access to her all the time becoming absurd.

"My feet ache, where can I sit?" I long to tell her she can rest wherever she pleases, but not in my father's chair. Already on edge and ready to snap, the last thing I needed was to hurt someone in the family when we were so close to paradise. Without hesitation, I tug her towards my usual seating area by the window. She sinks down into the reclining chair with a heave of relief, fidgeting around with all the buttons on the armrests. Dropping to my knees, I grasp her feet while she fights me away.

"We talked about this in the car, Elena. Let me live out my fantasies with you." Her eyes narrow as she simultaneously takes a bite out of her sandwich.

"You're not my slave. My feet will feel better, Anna. Get off the floor." I shake my head as I continue kneading her feet with care. Her stern expression lightens and I smile contentedly, happy that I can make her feel so good.

"You have no idea how happy it makes me to spoil you, Elena." I exclaim before lifting one of her feet up to brush my lips against it like an offering of worship. She gasps softly, looking at me in wonderment.

"I don't know if I'll ever get used to this, Anna. But for now, I'm trying." She mumbles quietly before peering back down at me expectantly - wishing her to let me love her.

22

Elena

I'm sitting opposite Antonio, Anna's father, and wishing I'd chosen a different seat. Anna quickly stores my shoes in the cabin and offers me a blanket. Aberto and Angelo soon appear with their wives and are led to the bedroom, where they'll remain with Antonio's 'play-things' during the journey. As Angelo takes his place beside his father he throws me a contemptuous glare.

"Women belong in the back," he snaps, struggling to buckle his seatbelt with his bandaged hand, wincing as he does so. A malicious grin forms on my face as I'm pleased to see him suffer.

Angelo looks to his father who refuses to make eye contact with me. "She's the female in their relationship which means she should be seated in the back with all the other women."

Anna rises as if she would like to cut out his tongue, but I rest a calming hand on hers telling her to stay still.

"Elena will sit wherever she chooses. Anna is my

daughter alone and will always follow Elena wherever she goes. I want to spend time with all of you, especially Anna as this will be the last time we see one another. My wife narrows her eyes and opens her mouth in astonishment.

"Father, I don't understand. I thought we were traveling together? That we'd remain together throughout this?"

"Anna, the second this plane departs, I'm a wanted man. Nowhere close to you. They'll come after me first and my dearest three children will be collateral loss afterwards. We have to part ways. Anna and Elena, you will get off at the destination first. Once you step off this plane Anna, you'll never see us again. That's how it must be." Anna gasps sharply but she does not argue back. Instead, her head hangs down as she attempts to hide the tears that fill her eyes. Not only am I losing tonight--my heart shatters for my wife. To comfort her, I need to make sure she knows that I will always remain beside her; clasping her hand in mine, I give it a gentle massage while she looks up at me, putting on a brave front. Anna is not as tough as she may seem; emotions still linger and she's my wife--I'll stay with her through thick and thin.

"You own me in every way, Anna. I'll never leave you." My promise to her followed by Angelo's snappy comment-- but Aberto approaches from behind taking her other hand into his, sitting beside her.

"Let us enjoy this time together, as a family. I will miss you greatly, lil sis." He leans in placing a sweet kiss on her forehead before hugging her while I try withdrawing my hand--however she holds onto me tighter than ever before, allowing herself to enjoy an embrace from her brother. At this sight I offer her a warm smile permitting her to clutch me as long as possible while enjoying the moment with Antonio who stares out the window observing the pilot boarding and the flight attendants shutting down the entrance and readying for take-off.

"Mr. Stonewell..."

"It's Antonio to you, Elena." He quickly corrects without looking at me, his eyes still fixed on the window. Angelo glares at me momentarily. Something about him makes me think he'd betray his family in a heartbeat. Ignoring his gaze, I know Anna is watching me and so I adjust my question accordingly.

"Antonio," I correct myself, "You said Anna is much like yourself. In what way?" His attention shifts back to me and his eyes lock with mine.

"How Anna captured you is the same way I captured her mother. It was love at first sight for both of us. It never mattered if she didn't feel the same or if she ran from me; I had given her my heart the moment our eyes met and I wasn't letting go. Now look at yourself; you're a queen now, a Stonewell. Anna will worship you until your dying breath; she'll give up her life for yours. You are in a position that women would die to be in." His words are true; did Anna even give Samantha the satisfaction of that final phone call? In truth, I don't even want to know.

"Take care of my daughter, Elena. Don't let my baby go a day without knowing she's loved." His beautiful eyes, I can see the pain in them; he loves his daughter and is doing this for her. I nod, my body too exhausted to cry. He looks away from me, not wanting anyone to witness the hurt in his eyes. Antonio is a man who never appears to break. The pilot announces our departure and I close my eyes as the plane moves down the runway, preparing to lift off. This is it; this is my new life with a woman that desires me more than anything else. I am scared yet exhilarated, ready to start this journey with my wife. Like Antonio, I keep my gaze on the window as we race along the tarmac until we leave the ground, sealing our fate; all of us have accepted our deal with death.

My destiny is with Anna now, and I'll stay with her until I take my last breath. Antonio takes a deep breath and I can see it in his eyes; he knows his fate is sealed. If I have children, they will know of Antonio and the sacrifices he made for Anna.

Once we are at flight level, I unbuckle my belt and cover myself with a blanket from the overhead bin, tucking my feet under me. When Anna notices my fatigue, she releases my hand and Angelo rises to go to the bar. The aircraft is quiet as our minds ponder the looming future ahead of us. A loving smile crosses her lips and almost takes my breath away – I close my eyes, drifting off to sleep.

Six hours later, I wake surprised we are still in-flight. Where are we going? Groggily, I sit up and before I can look her way, she's already holding a drink out for me.

"Here, baby. Drink this." But I shake my head at her and push the drink away then stand, stretching.

"I need to go to the bathroom." Anna stands too and Angelo huffs loudly.

"The girl can't even pee in peace." He snarls, glaring at me. What is his problem now? Anna takes my hand and pulls me away from Angelo's harsh words. I can feel his gaze on my back as we walk away. She takes me to a small private bathroom that surprises me with its size and closes the door behind her, locking it. I furrow my brows, "Anna, what the heck are you doing? c'mon, let me use the bathroom." She doesn't move but instead hops onto the sink. I sigh and pull my pants down and do my business. Once I'm finished relieving myself, I go to wash my hands only to be greeted by her voice. "I wasn't expecting this, Elena. I thought we would all live together under one roof and finish out our days as a family." Her gaze soften as she looks up at me.

"Does it bother you now that you are stuck with only me?" A hint of tease laces my voice as a playful smirk lines my lips.

"I'll have fun spanking your ass for that comment once we reach our marital home." I roll my eyes at her playfulness before turning serious again "It has nothing to do with that, Elena. It's just that knowing that we have to separate means we aren't truly free from the men who want us dead. We'll be looking over our shoulders for the rest of our lives." My breath catches as I stare into her worried face.

"I didn't know Elena. I had no idea that our safety was in jeopardy. I thought leaving would be the end of it." I turn off the water and embrace her between her legs, locking her tight in my arms.

"I don't care about the danger; what matters to me is us and our future together—our forever."

"We could experience lots of struggles, Elena. But I swear on my life that I won't let anything ever happen to you. I need you to know how much I love you." Our lips press together with a passionate, desperate kiss that professes our unending adoration for one another.

"I can hardly wait to be settled in our new home and make a life with you. There are so many things I want to try with you—to show you how much I love you." Her expression remains solemn.

"I need you to learn how to fight too, Elena. So, you're ready for whatever comes next." She still appears worried which means this is intense business. Gently cupping her face, I bring our foreheads together and look deep into her eyes.

"Then teach me, Anna—just don't ever lose your love

for me; because without it, I'm afraid of what will happen to me."

"That will never happen, Elena—and not just for now, but until the end of time." A faint smile fills my face as I look at her lovingly.

"Okay then, let's go sit with your father so you don't miss any more time with him." She flashes me a grin before stealing one last ardent kiss from me and finally releasing me.

23

———

Anna

After a few refueling stops, we finally arrive at our destination. We had to fly longer than usual, as my father intended to distract his watchers and make them believe we are on vacation. We de-board the plane and our luggage is loaded into a car. My father envelopes me in his arms, something he hasn't done since I was a little girl before my mother's death. I can't understand it all, but I know this means goodbye forever.

"You'll board the yacht and it will take you away. I'll never make contact or see you again. But let me tell you that I love you. Anna, I know I've been an asshole towards you; I'm sorry sweetheart, I should have been a better father to you." Tears begin flowing from my eyes, and after he step back, the weight of his words overwhelms me completely. I break down sobbing like a baby. He cups my face tightly, shaking me gently.

"You can do this Anna. I trained you for this fight. You have spent your entire life preparing for it. I may not win, and neither may your brothers, but you will. Believe in yourself," he says as he embraces me, planting a loving kiss on my forehead before boarding the plane. As I turn away and head towards the car, Elena waits at the passenger door for me to join her. I take one last look at the airplane as its engines roared; the doors close and it starts to take off. I have Elena now, and that is all that I need. Getting inside the car, I pull her close, cradling her close to me while we ride to our new home at the docks. I carry with me the map, keys, money, and passports with our new identities – though Elena doesn't bother looking at any of them, she finds comfort in my arms.

Once we arrive at the docks, Elena climbs out, pouting due to my popping her hand a few times for trying to carry our luggage. However, she gasps when she saw the yacht, smiling at me. I attempt to smile back and remain strong for Elena; though I ache from just losing my family, I did not regret my decision. I had Elena, my lovely wife. She follows me onto the boat while I tip the driver as I place our bags down. Trained as a child in nautical operations, I pull the map from my back pocket and scowl at Elena as she explores the boat. We are to sail for two days before reaching our destination- someplace remote and isolated- allowing us time away from society. Then, I depart ahead of schedule, not wanting to be on land too long.

Sitting with me, Elena clutches onto me nervously while I steer the yacht far enough offshore so that we are out of sight from land. The boat is already full of supplies, and more than enough fuel to last us. She holds me close as I navigate us away from civilization until sunset and we stop for rest. After teaching Elena how to lower the anchor, we both make our way down to the bedroom where Elena quickly undresses and showers with me joining shortly after.

"I'm sorry for all this, Elena. You didn't ask for this." She gazes up at me with water dripping from her hair as the shower head roars above us.

"Anna, I don't have any regrets. All that matters to me is that I have you." She smiles and caresses my body with gentle hands, licking her lips afterward. Then the shower shuts off and she leads me out of the bathroom.

"Make love to me, Anna; there's no one else here now. You can spoil me any way you want; I'm yours. Every part of me belongs to you." Damnit! Why now? I swallow hard, opening my eyes wide to process what she just said. My gaze slides down to her beautiful breasts and then I give in. Drawing her close, I crush my lips against hers in an electrifying kiss. I kiss her until she's breathless, then push her onto the bed, swiftly climbing on top of her. She opens her legs for me, squeezing my ass firmly as I press into her.

"Take what you want from me, Anna. Show me who I belong to." The air crackles with electric energy as my love transforms into a passionate vixen for me. I capture her lips eagerly, our tongues dancing together with wild abandon back and forth. Our bodies brush together, creating a rhythm that I can't help but moan in pleasure at. With each moment that passes, the sex between us gets better and better. I break away from the kiss with reluctance before flipping her onto her stomach, pulling her against me. She knows exactly what I need and starts grinding against me, pushing her ass from side to side, sparking intense pleasure in my body until I can no longer resist the urge to let go. My body trembles as I reach my orgasm while she takes advantage of my weakness, quickly turning around and pushing me down on the bed as if she was possessed by an unquenchable hunger for me. She hungrily dives between my legs, her tongue plunging inside me repeatedly until finally I scream out in ecstasy, my entire body shaking just the way she wanted it to shake. I love her so much. I will never let this end.

And suddenly, all of my worries vanish; just like that - she has made all my troubles disappear. It's a temporary solution, but one I needed, because I simply want to hold my wife and love her. Knowing how much she wanted to take care of me meant everything to me. She grants me grace, straddling me, placing her body on top of mine, letting me hold her for as long as I needed her.

"I love you, Elena," I murmur. She leans into me, then smiles playfully before giving me a soft kiss on the lips.

"I love you too, Anna. This is forever."

"Forever," I reply in agreement.

24

Elena

Six months later

Anna places a pistol in my hands, aiding me to aim the firearm at the cans she has set up a few yards away. We have been on this island for six months with endless days of training and sex. I'm exhausted, yet Anna's talents make me feel as though I'm being trained by an experienced fighter. Little did I know that she was this skilled. It's almost like she's a trained killer.

Spending this time with her alone on the island, I've been able to get to know Anna better. She told me how her father sent her away every summer, and how she couldn't understand why she was forced to train to protect herself all the time. And it appears Antonio was right all along, she was going to need to learn how to protect herself one day.

"Elena, focus on your target," she breathes close to my neck, her hands resting on my waist and kissing it gently.

"How am I supposed to focus when you're doing this?! I'm ready to take my clothes off, not kill!" Anna chuckles and steps back from me.

"If you miss, then I get to have my way with you," She stares at me intently for a moment before returning my attention to the target.

"And if I don't miss?" Anna smiles alluringly again.

"Then you get your way with me." I point the gun at the cans and intentionally shoot wildly because what I want is to miss my target—I love when Anna fucks me, and goodness gracious, she has been holding back on me with her incredible love making skills. The way she ravishes my pussy now, I yearn for her like food after starvation. I miss and whirl around to face her, put down the weapon in the manner she showed me and leave it on the ground. She looks at me mischievously.

"Elena, this practice is important. Was that shot on purpose?" I shrug nonchalantly and roll my eyes towards her direction.

"Did you tempt me with sex just so I would miss?" Anna grins flirtatiously at me while bending over to pick up the gun.

"Bedroom, NOW." She growls and I saunter past her, swaying my hips, feeling my entire body inflames with anticipation for what's to come. As I enter our small beach house, she swiftly kicks off her shoes and delightedly chases me up to the bedroom. We both melt into each other's arms and she gives my ass a gentle squeeze.

"Alright, Elena, you win." She plants a loving kiss on my lips that sends sparks of electricity throughout my whole being. I loop my arms around her neck as she pushes me onto the bed and, in no time at all, I find myself stripped of my clothes. Every time we make love it feels like the first time, reigniting the passion from our first night together.

Holding both my wrists above my head with her hands, she looks down at me and whispers between kisses:

"I love you, Elena."

"I love you more." I reply quickly, then help her shed her clothing as eagerly as I ache to feel her skin against mine.

"Keep your hands above your head, or I'll tie you to the bed," I grin, biting my lip as her mouth travels down my body. She grips my breasts, teasing me with licks and suckles while she lightly bites at them. I moan unconsciously and arch my back, attempting to obey her orders. Her hands explore further; eventually landing between my legs.

"I'm going to fuck your pussy, then I'm going to eat it, Elena." I whimper when she slides two fingers inside me, thrusting in and out of me.

"Always wet for me, Elena. I love you so fucking much." Anna utters, making me moan again as she curls her digits around me, moving them side to side and swirling them around before thrusting in and out of me once more. My desire quickly mounts until I'm screaming out her name in ecstasy as she drives her fingers in and out of me, coaxing out every ounce of pleasure from my orgasm. She swiftly spreads my legs wider then buries her head between them like a ravenous animal - it's as if we've explored each other's bodies so much over the past six months that Anna knows exactly how to make me come hard and fast. The waves of pleasure leave me weakly gripping the sheets, fighting the urge to grasp onto her as they ebb away...

Anna loves to pleasure me with her mouth, and she'd spend all day between my legs if I let her. My toes curl and my hips buck as she swipes her tongue over my wetness, teasing my clit before driving it deep inside of me. I come hard against her until I can't take it anymore, screaming as my hips gyrate wildly, my eyes rolling into the back of my head from the intensity of the orgasm that rocks through me as she thrusts her tongue in and out of me again and again. Her hands caress my body, moving away from between my legs to pepper me with loving kisses, before returning to tease my breasts again and I can't take it anymore. She chuckles when I cup her face, pulling her into a tender kiss and pouring all of my love into her. She melts into me, spreading my legs further apart and grinding against me, moaning into my mouth.

"You broke the rules, Elena. Looks like I have to tie you up." I smirk, not caring about any rules.

"Whatever." I respond playfully, pulling her into another deep passionate kiss, trying to forget our troubles for just one moment, wanting only to feel her and enjoy being with my wife.

"I love you, Anna. I'm yours forever," I vow to her tenderly. She kisses me again and a kissed-induced smile lights up her face as she reaches under the bed for the fur cuffs, ready to take me in completely. My lips twitch with anticipation, eager to give her full control over my body. This is what we need—to savor our time together now so that when we're off to war, we can fight side by side until our last breaths. I'm bonded with Anna until death.

To be continued.....

ABOUT THE AUTHOR

Jenna Kent

Jenna Kent, coffee lover, and book lover of all things romance with a sweet spot for masculine dominant femmes resides in Wayne Michigan, just about 20 miles from Detroit, Michigan. Jenna is a steamy lesbian romance author of fast-paced instalove romance. Expect them to be over-the-top, absurdly ridiculous–but always with a happy ending.

Would you like a free steamy romance book by Jenna Kent? Download here:

https://BookHip.com/QMFLQSW

Check my link in bio for more info!

https://linktr.ee/jennakentbooks

Subscribe to my newsletter!

subscribepage.io/QNoPd8

Instagram @jennakentauthor